# HYBRID MISFIT

## THE MISFITS #1

## EVE LANGLAIS

## PROLOGUE

ADULTS. Ugh. Always claiming the shit they forced on you was for your own good. Take the treatments they subjected me to, for instance.

*The medicine will make you better. Those gazillion needles will improve your quality of life.* How, by granting me a career as a pin cushion? Hell, some of the stuff they siphoned into my veins glowed. It was a wonder I could sleep at night with all the wacky shit they filled me with.

But the battery of tests and treatments weren't the only things I had to contend with. I was a prisoner. A patient. A test subject. Those in charge explained the locked doors to our rooms were so we wouldn't wander at night or get into trouble. The barbed-wire fencing around the compound, again, for our protection, to keep the wild animals out—funny since some of the wildest creatures were held within. As for the guards, they were for our safety. Safety against what? It wasn't as if they stopped those doctors when they strapped us down and poisoned us with their certainly-not-FDA-approved cocktails.

So many of us died from those treatments. Those lucky bastards. Others emerged from the agony and screaming changed. How I tired of averted eyes when they said it wouldn't hurt, even as molten fire burned through our veins.

Liars.

Bastards.

*Meat...*

For every one of us that died, for every one of us that cried, and for every one of us that lost our humanity, someone would pay. Make that someone would die, not by my hand, for, even with the torture I'd suffered at their hands, I lacked that kind of ruthlessness. But my brothers and sisters, made kin by the shared experimentation, they had no such qualms—in fact, they craved violence. They reveled in death.

When the uprising occurred, blood rained down and soaked the earth. Like a volcano erupting, vengeance, too long bottled, burst forth with deadly consequence. In the deep of night, when only bogeymen—and test subjects— dared walk, I ran with the flames of Hades reaching high behind me in the dark sky. As I escaped my prison and the adopted siblings who'd finally turned on me with covetous eyes, I heard the chilling screams of the liars as retribution came back to bite them.

Then to eat them.

As for me, I fled and hid, but most of all, I rejoiced because I was finally free.

## CHAPTER 1

APPARENTLY, someone forgot to mention that with freedom came responsibility. Escaping the gated institution I'd lived in for three long years didn't make everything all better. I didn't get an instant happily-ever-after. But life was definitely better.

I certainly didn't miss the barrage of needles, the loneliness of being locked away, and the communal showers with the other girls.

On the other hand, though, I'd have to say I wasn't too crazy about the gnawing pain in my stomach or sleeping on the cold, hard ground.

Freedom wasn't comfortable. It also forced me to face some crucial facts. I needed a place to live. Clothes. I needed sustenance to survive. For all this, I needed a job.

Of course, that was easier said than done, especially considering I had a definite lack of skills. A grade twelve education did not make me a rocket scientist, although I could still recite by rote some of the Spanish I'd learned, but somehow counting to ten in another language didn't impress the prospective employees who interviewed me.

I had no marketable skills—unless screaming at a high pitch while writhing counted. While in captivity, we'd had no access to computers or technology, and books were doled out for good behavior. I'm afraid to say, I didn't read often.

Emerging into the real world like a butterfly from a chrysalis, I needed to learn how to fly. Or, at the very least, type and fluently speak a second language. It wasn't as if I didn't have any skills, but somehow, I didn't think peeing in a cup with no hands would gain me points on a job application.

I tried all the easy places first—McDonalds, Walmart, and other retailers that paid minimum wage and required no experience. Nobody hired me. I wasn't sure why. Was there something in my eyes that frightened them? Could they sense my otherness?

No one ever said. And I couldn't find the words to ask.

Annoyed that the world seemed determined to foil my plan to start a new life, I moped for days and thought about going back to kill the managers who couldn't see my potential. A little revenge would have helped with my hunger at least, but caution stayed my hand—and a squeamishness over parts of my diet that forced me to resort to hunting those of my kind—well, my kind until I'd changed that was. *Don't go there.* Don't think about it because the loss of my innocence and humanity remained a memory I preferred not to dwell on.

So what should a girl of twenty-one with good teeth, no skills, or advanced education do for money? Where could I work and have access to a gullible food source?

Say hello to Trixi, the newest exotic dancer at XXXButts—not one of the more upscale clubs like Bunny Tails, but not the bottom of the heap like Dollar Dancing.

Frown and disapprove all you want. I could handle it. There was no denying I'd chosen to work in a shocking environment, replete with chrome, mirrors, and lots of naked women. I wouldn't deny that what some of the men said or expected of us was degrading to women, but in the club's defense, they paid really fucking well. They paid on time. But most important of all, they made feeding my hungers—and not the meat and potato variety —so much easier.

XXXButts was just a starting point, though. Those first few years after my escape, I moved often, fleeing sometimes with only the clothes on my back when members of my past caught up to me and learned, to their detriment, that I preferred to stay hidden and out of their clutches.

During those hard learning years, I lost my squeamishness. I had to or die. The new me adopted the new motto of "I will kill to survive." Word must have spread, or the numbers against me diminished, because, eventually, I managed to stop running. I settled in a spot, made myself a home, probably because I discovered, to my amazement, that I wasn't the only *special girl* working at the newest club. Of course, the siren and werebunny didn't come close to my state of being, but because of our differences—and in spite of them—we forged a friendship that was stronger for our specialness.

My unique appeal on stage caught the attention of a bigger club within months—I knew how to please a crowd. Dragging my friends along with me, we moved to the more upscale location, and I landed the cushy feature dancer position while Lana and Claire landed jobs as shot girl and waitress. My success entitled us to the best shifts, the cleanest, most secure lockers, and a never-ending flow of cash—among other things.

During my time on stage, I enticed and enflamed. I swung on the pole in a titillating dance as the featured Saturday night dancer. When I shook my booty, all eyes in the place were glued to me. What could I say? I was hot, and not only did I know it, but the humans did, too. Even better, their slack-jawed excitement fed a part of me without my even touching them. If only I could have fed my other hunger hands-free.

My friends and I settled into a comfortable routine. We exchanged life stories. We watched out for each other, and I thrived.

I should have known my comfortable existence wouldn't last.

Premonition didn't warn me as I hung upside down on a pole, my ankles crisscrossed while my anaconda thighs gripped the upright bar. My hands cupped my breasts—which were barely hidden by my sequined pasties—while my hips dry humped the steel support. Multitasking at its best. I was in the midst of my routine, sucking in all the thick, sexual energy permeating the air, when they walked in.

Shit. Fuck. Damn. A litany of curse words went through my mind when I saw them, my long-lost brothers. Or should I say rejected lovers—although, given their rough ways, many would have said rapists—because, after the change, I went from little sister to coveted object.

Their appearance couldn't bode well. I pretended not to notice them, hoping I'd get lucky and they wouldn't recognize me.

Their freakish yellow eyes zeroed in on me immediately, shooting down that wishful thought. I hid my own special eyes behind contacts lenses of dull brown. Apparently, violet-colored eyes, ones that appeared to light up from within, weren't the norm for humans. Imagine that.

Although I wore a mundane human disguise, I couldn't mask my scent, and I could see my lost brethren sniffing the air as they took seats close to the stage. They didn't make it to the pervert row, that first rank around the stage where leering men sat with eager faces and enjoyed the up close and personal show. But the trio didn't sit far behind, and I could see them muttering to each other, even if I couldn't hear their words over the blaring rock music.

*Probably plotting ways of capturing me so they can drag me back to their lair for devious torture.*

Okay, that was a tad melodramatic. They probably didn't have a lair, but I wasn't kidding about the capture part. They wanted me because of what I could do. Or, should I say, what my blood was capable of.

I had no intention of becoming some kind of blood bank for them, even though I was tired of always looking over my shoulder. Freedom was worth dying for. I would never allow myself to become a prisoner, an object at the mercy of others, again.

My set ended with me bent over and exposing parts of me that should never see daylight—it didn't bother me, though. I truly had no inhibitions when it came to displaying my body.

As soon as I could, I rushed to the back of the stage and slipped behind the curtain. I figured I didn't have much time before they came looking, but I needed at least a minute to change out of my glittery outfit into something more respectable for walking the city streets. There were probably some who'd argue that the micro mini I shrugged on, along with the sheer blouse and high heels, was no better. Too bad.

After the sterile whites I'd worn for years—asexual garments that smelled of bleach—I craved color and loved to look sexy. Besides, it made getting dinner so much easier. I often liked to grab a snack to tide me over before going in to work.

But tonight, I wished I'd worn running shoes instead of three-inch heels as I slipped out the back door, usually manned by Bernie, our bouncer. Tonight, the gorilla whom I bummed gum from wasn't standing at his usual post, probably because he'd been beheaded and his body had been partially stuffed into the dumpster. Poor Bernie, his face still bore an expression of surprise as his head swung from a fist. My eyes followed the hand up the arm to a familiar face.

So much for my plan of sneaking out.

At five-foot-ten, lanky, and with a shock of platinum

hair, my ex-brother still wore the sneer he'd been famous for back in the institution.

"Jonathon," I greeted him carefully. "Long time no see." And I could have done with a lot longer, given the last time I'd seen him he'd had his pants around his ankles and a bleeding nose. I still fondly remembered the conversation he had with the edge of my fist.

His attempted rape earned him solitary at the institution, and I lost my pudding at dinner—a huge bummer at the time.

After the uprising, I never saw him again, although I'd had chance encounters over the years with others. They weren't happy family reunions, needless to say, but I was proud to say I'd always come out on top.

"Love the new name, *Trixi*." Jonathon coughed up a nasty chuckle as he recited the fluffy name I'd given myself, but seriously, who wanted an exotic dancer called Beth? Besides, as far as I was concerned, Beth had died along with my old life. The new me didn't like to remember the humanity I'd lost.

"What brings you to town?" I asked while unobtrusively scanning the darkness of the alley for his two companions.

"This and that," he answered vaguely. "You know, the whole crew has missed you. I know they'd love to see you again." His yellow eyes narrowed as he smiled at me with pronounced canines.

*Why what sharp teeth you have.* An aspect of Jonathon's curse, along with an allergy to sunlight.

"I'll just bet you've missed me. How is your nose?" I might have smirked as I asked.

"Still as mouthy as ever, I see. We'll have to fix that."

Him and what army? I wouldn't go down easy. "What do you want?"

The smile on his lips was more chilling than the expression in his eyes. "You."

Shudder. It didn't take a genius to realize he and his friends probably whacked off to visions of me naked, cuffed, and spread eagle, a fleshy buffet for them to feed on.

I decided to stop wasting time with idle chitchat. Any idiot could tell this wasn't a social call. Besides, attacking Jonathon would probably draw the other two out. Not bad odds for someone special like me—and I was hungry, having skipped out on work early before fully feeding.

I turned it on, the half of me that fascinated men, the side that drew them with a sensual allure they couldn't resist. Say hello to my succubus side. "Mmm, I see someone still has fantasies about what could have been. Wanna play?" With a sensual smile that promised delight, I sashayed toward Jonathon, the hypnotic sway of my body capturing him and allowing me to approach.

My brothers considered themselves predators—the baddest bunch around. Ha, they looked like amateurs compared to me. After all, I was the only one who'd gotten both sides of the curse—and lived. Perhaps I had an inflated sense of my worth, but then again, so far the score was Trixi, fifteen, and bad guys, zero.

Held under my sensual spell, Jonathon could only blink as I neared him. The nails on the tips of my fingers extended into claws—really sharp and deadly ones. My canines—a present from my other, more sinister half—

also descended as my adrenaline ramped up in anticipation of the violence I was about to unleash.

Time to open a can of whoop ass.

Close now, I leaned toward Jonathon, inhaling his scent, only to wrinkle my nose. Ugh, he stank. Not physically, but metaphysically, the experimentation doing to him what only death does to humans—stripping his soul, his very aura. Without it, he smelled of decay, the sickly sweet scent of the grave, even as his body appeared intact. Yet, even without his soul, my succubus powers worked on him, but in his case, I'd feed on his very life, the spark that animated him—though not for much longer.

Bad smell or not, former brother in torture or not, he needed to die before he could tell others he'd seen me. I liked my new life and my friends, thank you very much. I wouldn't let him and his covetous nature ruin it for me.

I pressed against him, my mouth opening and preparing to suck the life—putrid as it was—right out of him.

"Now," Jonathon croaked, managing to force the word out through the enthralling spell I'd placed him under.

How surprising. Usually, once I had them under my spell, they couldn't move until I released them.

My brethren had grown stronger. Not a reassuring thought given the situation.

The sound of several thumps hitting the ground behind me forced my hand—and deprived me of dinner. With a quick, slicing slash, I opened up Jonathon's throat before he could raise a hand to defend himself. I'd lost my fear of violence after my escape when I realized it was kill or be killed. As Jonathon sagged to the ground, leaving the wall he leaned against bare, I whirled and pressed my back against the rough concrete.

It would seem I had miscalculated. Jonathon might have entered the club with only two lackeys, but facing me were a half-dozen faces, of which I only recognized two.

Who were these strangers? And a better question, were they vamps like my experimental brothers?

My question was quickly answered. With a snarl that showed a lot of pointed teeth, they dove on me. Deciding the bottom of the pile wasn't a good position for me—I preferred to ride my bucking men—I sprang into the air, calling forth my tarnished wings, which burst from my back in a shower of fluffy grey feathers. I was a woman with many hidden talents.

At the apex of my leap, I flapped my wings, to no avail. Gravity pulled me down with the help of a tall attacker, who wrapped his hands around my ankle, acting as an anchor keeping me grounded.

Pump my wings as I might, my free foot kicking at the restraining hands, I couldn't break free, and the whole gang joined in pulling me down.

A piercing shriek escaped me, not of maidenly distress but rage.

*How dare they!*

I'd suffered as much as they. We should have shared a bond. We should have banded together against those who tortured and changed us. Instead, because I'd turned out different than all of them, they thirsted for me.

Unfair. I just wanted my freedom and to be left

alone. Simple needs that would prove impossible if I let them get away with news of my continuing existence. I stopped my attempts to escape and let myself suddenly fall, my unexpected capitulation sending them stumbling.

As I hit the ground, I moved. My fist shot out and jabbed the one who'd clipped my wings, the diaphragm shot bending him over to gasp. Even if they were no longer human, one thing remained the same—they still needed to breathe.

Hulking bodies with glowing yellow eyes and gnashing teeth moved in to crowd me. That wouldn't do at all. I needed breathing room to lay down the law —*my law*.

My wings retracted as I spun and kicked out, my high-heeled foot hitting and sinking into soft flesh. For a moment, my stiletto stuck, but a vicious yank set my foot free, and the figure slumped to the ground gushing blood.

Ew. I'd ruined my shoes. This evening was getting worse all the time.

A blow from behind snapped my head forward, but I'd been hit harder than that before—the hospital staff didn't know the word gentle—and before I'd even brought my head back up, my foot kicked backwards like a pissed donkey and connected with some soft male parts. His squeal brought a grim smile to my lips.

My fists were also busy, driving forward, claws extended, to rip and punch with bloody effect.

The problem with fighting others like me, though, was the rate at which we healed. Even as I took one down, the first bounced up again, his eyes burning and his lips pulled back over snarling teeth.

I had to admit it wasn't looking good for me, but I refused to give up. Even if they managed to take me down and capture me, I'd never stop fighting. I'd learned one important lesson while in that prison shrouded under the guise of a hospital. Freedom was the most precious thing I could own, and by damn, I wouldn't allow anyone to take that from me again, not without a vicious fight.

Slugging left and right, kicking back and forth, covered in a sticky layer of blood, I wasn't aware the tide of the battle had changed until the body I fought fell over and I discovered there was nothing left to hit. And yet, the sound of someone's fist hitting flesh still filled the air. Except it wasn't mine.

I pivoted in time to see the last of my attackers drop, laid flat by a giant of a man, and I mean giant.

My lips parted to say thank you, but the words became caught in my throat as eyes glowing the green of fresh spring grass rose to meet mine. For once, I was the one spellbound.

My breath caught, my lower extremities heated, and my lips parted on a sigh. I couldn't see the face of my sparring partner, the gloom of the alley hung too deep, but I didn't care because, sinking into the green depths of his eyes, I felt a calming peace—and a naughty thrill. I took a step toward him, or I meant to, but my legs buckled. I sank to my knees, my mind fuzzy with incomprehension.

*Am I injured?* I didn't recall receiving any severe wounds.

Peeking down at myself, I noted the blood staining my clothes and skin. I vaguely felt the sting and throb of dozens of scratches and bruises, none of them grievous enough to cause such a weakness. The needle, however, sticking out of my side explained a lot.

"Fuckers," I slurred before keeling forward on my face.

## CHAPTER 2

Yawn. Stretch. I awoke in a bed—a nice, fluffy, soft one. And so totally not mine.

Now you might think, being part succubus, that I woke in strange beds all the time. Not true. Sleepovers implied intimacy and trust. I never indulged in either.

Thus, finding myself at someone's mercy meant I sprang out of the bed in a flash, instinct placing me in front of a wall while my eyes scanned the room I found myself in.

As rooms went, it was actually quite nice...and confusing.

*Did I die and go to heaven?*

A valid question, given everything around me—from the sheets to the walls to the rugs—gleamed a snowy white, including the T-shirt covering my body—a huge tent of material that hung down to my knees. The reassuring feel of my thong between my cheeks and lack of labial soreness led me to believe that, despite my undressed—or considering what I usually wore, dressed

—state, I was unmolested. But that begged the question...

"What the fuck?"

"Maybe later," replied a deep voice that shot a shiver right down to my toes, but especially lingered in my crotch.

I whirled and beheld a behemoth—a handsome one, but still a freaking beast of a man. He towered over me, and thick muscles stretched the fabric of the—you guessed it—white T-shirt he wore. His thighs strained the seams of his jeans, and peeking down, I noted the size of his bare feet—extra freaking large.

He was handsome in a square-jawed, nose-flattened-by fists kind of way—in other words, a brute of a man. The most shocking feature of his appearance, though, if one ignored his size, was his hair. White and tinged with the blue of an iceberg in the northern seas, it stood in spikes on his crown, but despite its pale color, he appeared to be in his early thirties.

My arousal woke with a sensual purr, tightening my nipples and moistening my cleft. He was so totally my type, which made me distrust him right off the bat. "Who the hell are you?"

"Funny, I was going to ask you the same thing." His green eyes twinkled, and even without the glow, I recognized them.

"You're the guy who helped me out last night." Which didn't make him a good guy in my books—yet. But it did mean I'd give him a chance to prove he didn't have nefarious intentions toward my body before I killed him. Or I'd let him fuck me. Either way, I'd ensure I came out on top. I was never one to look a gift horse—as in hung—in the mouth, not when I could be on my knees. "Why did you fight them?" Altruism and Good Samaritans usually stayed far away from the kind of violence I faced.

He shrugged, a nonchalant roll of a massive shoulder. "I needed the exercise."

Big, handsome, and modest. I wondered what flaw he hid.

"Thanks," I said, the word emerging grudgingly. Having survived on my own for so long, it galled me to admit his aid had saved my ass from the proverbial frying pan, but the warmth in his gaze let me know I hadn't escaped the fire yet.

"Thanks for what? If they hadn't played dirty with the tranquilizer, I do believe you'd have flattened them on your own."

Heat warmed my cheeks at his praise. I almost choked at the sensation.

What an utterly ridiculous and girly reaction. Since when did that happen?

My smile transformed into a scowl, which only deepened his grin. "Who are you, and where am I?" I asked in a grumpy tone that had a lot to do with the reaction of my body to his presence, but for my peace of mind, I'd blame on a lack of coffee.

"My name is Simon, and you're in my loft on the twelfth floor," he said, his voice a low, soothing rumble that I enjoyed way too much.

Good manners dictated I introduce myself, even if I still remained unsure of the situation—besides, in case we ended up naked in bed, he'd need a name to bellow when

I gave him the best orgasm of his life. "My name is Beth." I almost slapped a hand over my mouth when my old name came flying out as natural as you please. I must have looked shocked, for he tilted his head.

"Beth. It's much nicer than your stage name, I must say."

"How do you know about that?"

The giant chuckled. "You had Trixi labeled inside your clothes, so unless you like to wear other people's underwear and outfits, common sense dictates, along with the fact that I found you in the back alley of an exotic dancing location, that you have a stage name. If it makes you feel any better, Simon is my real name."

"What's your stage name?" I blurted out, curious.

Again, his lips curved into a smile that moistened my panties, and I had to wonder if he was an incubus because, quite honestly, despite all the men I'd enticed over the years, he was the first to return the favor.

"My stage name when I used to step into the ring was Puff."

I wrinkled my brow. "As in puff pastry?"

Again, he laughed, the low timbre of the sound reverberating throughout my body pleasantly. "No, as in Puff, the magic dragon." He'd really lost me at this point, and he must have noticed it because he snorted in amusement. "Don't worry. You'll figure out why soon enough. Now, what do you say to some breakfast?"

Hunger gnawed at me sudden like, and my mouth watered, but not for the bacon I smelled drifting through the open bedroom door. Looking him up and down, my eyes lingered on the distinct bulge in his pants. I licked my lips as I realized I could go for some *sausage*. Injuries always wakened my hungers.

Smiling at him, I turned on the juice to prep him for my idea of a morning pick-me-upper. "I'd love to *eat*, honey."

"Bad succubus," he chided. "Is that any way to thank your host?"

My jaw dropped as he outed me. Before I could ask him how he knew—and resisted me!—he walked away. The view proved surprisingly nice, especially for a guy his size. But I was allowing myself to get distracted.

How the hell had he known? Other than my two best friends from the club, I held my state of being a close secret.

*And how come he's not on his knees worshipping me with his tongue?* Surely I wasn't disappointed, but something made my lips twist in a moue of displeasure. Having never experienced rejection before, I quickly decided I didn't like it one bit.

I scurried after Simon, my bare feet sinking into the plush carpeting that ended outside the bedroom door. The gleaming wood floors—white pine, what else?—were chilly under my feet. Actually, his whole condo felt a tad cool, not that it bothered me. How hot or cold a body was remained a human concern. And I was far from human anymore.

I crossed the wide expanse of the living room, which shone bright and white, probably because of the wide bank of windows that stretched from the floor to the cathedral ceiling. Good thing my other side didn't suffer from the sunlight curse like my brothers. I was starting to wonder at his obsession with white, though. Would it kill him to have a little color?

A clanging of dishes alerted me to Simon's presence in the kitchen. The white kitchen—gee, did they forget color when they decorated?—opened into the living area, separated only by a gleaming island that was topped by—you guessed it—a white slab of marble.

I perched myself on the bar stool tucked under the breakfast bar and studied Simon as he plated some steaming food, the only spot of color in the whole place.

I wouldn't deny he was nice to watch. For such a big man, he moved light on his feet, and the play of his muscles under his clothing warmed me better than any coffee.

He didn't say a word as he finished making breakfast, but his eyes often shifted to me, along with a half-smile that made me want to smile back. I clamped my lips tight instead, not trusting how comfortable I found myself with this veritable stranger—whom I'd probably have to kill for guessing my secret. What a shame.

The silence stretched, as did my curiosity. Only once he handed me my portion on a huge plate heaped with enough food for three did I voice my question. "Why did you call me a succubus?"

In the process of shoveling food into his mouth—a fascinating process that made me flash to him devouring my pussy instead—he swallowed and took a sip of his orange juice before he answered me. "Haven't you figured it out yet? I'm not human, just like you."

His reply threw me, and I peered at him more closely. On the outside, he looked like a man—a drop-dead, gorgeously muscled one. I tuned in my other senses and sucked in my breath.

*What the hell is he?*

His aura glowed, thick and colorful, telling me without any words he'd not only lived a long life, but also a full one that ran the gamut from sweetness to violence. To me, a person's aura, their soul so to speak, appeared as a shroud around them. Over the years, I'd learned to read them—most of the time. The thicker the shroud, the older the person. Simon's was the thickest I'd ever seen.

Another neat thing I'd learned was that the colors of a person's soul told me what kind of life they'd lived. Darker colors stood for the violence and ugliness in a person's life while lighter colors represented happy times and caring for others. Most people tended to lean toward one shade or the other, however, Simon was a kaleidoscope, with all the colors of the rainbow plus some swirling in his super-thick shroud.

My mouth watered just looking at it, for he stirred the hunger of my succubus side. But unlike a true soul-sucking nymph, I could control myself and take what I needed without killing the provider. And, if the sexual energy around me ran high enough, I could feed without even touching. Hands-free was definitely not as yummy as the power fed to me via skin-to-skin contact, though.

"You have a pretty aura, but it doesn't tell me what you are." Although I did know whatever supernatural caste he belonged to was definitely long-lived.

"What does your other side tell you?" His eyes glittered, their faint glow pointing to his less-than-human DNA. And once again, he'd shocked me.

*How does he recognize what I am?*

I didn't like my other side as much and preferred not to wake that evil, sleeping giant, but once suggested, my darker side roused. My eyes narrowed, and my senses heightened. I inhaled deeply, my mind sorting through the myriad of smells from bacon, eggs, and toast to something old, musty, and...I faltered at the alienness that assailed my olfactory meter.

*What the fuck is he?*

He chuckled at my puzzled expression. "Okay, maybe you can't figure it out."

"So tell me?" I pinned him with my prize-winning—make that trouser-dropping—smile.

Over the wide counter, he leaned, close enough that if I tilted my head forward, our lips would touch. I almost did it, and I couldn't entirely blame my succubus nature. "Tell you? That would be too easy."

He smiled at me as he leaned back. He resumed eating his breakfast while I fumed. Okay, I was sulking. Having learned to use my attributes, I'd grown used to men—and yes, even women—doing as I asked.

Grumpy, I refused to look at him while I ate food that I swallowed without tasting. My mind raced through the possibilities and dismissed them. I arrived at the end of my short list of supernatural beings—a longer list than before my incarceration but by no means complete because, as I'd learned, the world held many secrets. The only conclusion I'd arrived at said he wasn't a vampire—his aura made that answer easy. But given my reaction to him—AKA my throbbing, wet crotch—he could be an incubus. Yet, while he drew me and made me want to indulge in carnal delights, I didn't get the impression that was the right answer.

*He's something else, but what?*

I studied him in silence, hunched over the breakfast bar, munching on toast. His eyes twinkled, but he didn't speak, too busy shoveling food in his mouth. A body like his probably required lots of calories to keep it going.

*Good boy. Eat up because you're going to need lots of energy for what I have planned.* My pussy just about hummed in agreement.

He finally broke the silence. "How old are you?"

"Why? How old do I look?" I replied with an enigmatic smile.

"Your very nature means you don't age, but I have to say, it's been a while since I've encountered one of your ilk. I'd thought you all dead in the last cleansing. How long have you been hiding?"

I gaped at him. "Say again? There are more of me? The doctors said I was the only one."

It was while we both stared at each other with puzzled faces that a swirling mist appeared behind him in the kitchen and coalesced into a man shape.

"Behind you," I yelled, throwing myself off the stool and diving over the sofa to crouch in a readied stance. I was ready to kick the ass of whoever had disrupted our breakfast.

"I smell something yummy," said a new masculine voice from right behind my ear. I would have shrieked, but the newcomer spun me and plastered his lips to mine.

And, to my surprise, I enjoyed it.

## CHAPTER 3

Enjoyable as I found the kiss, I stopped it by biting down on the tongue that insinuated itself between my lips. I had a moment to taste the sweetest blood ever before the man who'd embraced me pulled away.

Given my past experiences in these types of situations, I expected cursing. I even braced for a backhand. What I got, though, was laughter. Masculine chuckles erupted, and I relaxed at the realization that my actions wouldn't meet with violence—yet. I trusted no one, even someone who laughed with such ease.

As I looked upon the newcomer, I noted Simon ignored him as he continued to eat, working on my still-full plate.

Not as big or tall as my green-eyed savior, the stranger was definitely all male and handsome. In the white glare of the living space, his bald crown shone, and he posed with a hand on his hip as I perused him. I obliged, looking him up and down, liking what I saw.

Tanned skin tempted the chocolate lover in me.

Around his mouth was a short goatee, providing great friction I'd bet for when he buried his face between a woman's thighs. His eyes, exotically shaped, were an electric blue so clear they looked unreal. He wore loose-fitting trousers that snugged his lean waist but bunched at the ankles. Over his torso he wore a billowy white linen shirt, and in one ear hung a gold hoop. He looked like a bloody pirate, and given how my body still trembled at his stolen kiss, I now wished I'd let him shiver me with his timber.

I then looked at him more deeply, my esoteric side quivering at the sight, for I'd never seen an aura like his before. It kept twisting and changing shape and color, like a smoky rainbow that refused to stay still. It stirred my hunger, and I licked my lips, wondering what it would taste like.

The newcomer grinned at me, his smile wide and bright—a true poster boy for Colgate. "Simon, where did you find this delightful creature? I thought they were all killed back in the great cleansing."

I frowned. What was it with this cleansing thing they'd both mentioned? And how did they both see through my human guise to my true nature?

"I think she's new," rumbled Simon.

"New to what? Can someone explain to me what the hell you're talking about?" I said, placing my hands on my hips in exasperation. "And who the hell is this guy who looks like Mr. Clean's tanned brother?"

The mocha-skinned scoundrel in question swept me a courtly bow. "I, fair maiden, am Gene, prominent member of the Ifrit."

"The If what?"

"He's a Djinn," explained Simon, who'd finally finished eating and sank onto one of the white leather couches.

"You mean, like, a genie?" I giggled. I couldn't help it when I thought of the only examples of Djinn I'd ever seen. "I saw *Aladdin*. Isn't he supposed to be blue?"

Gene folded his arms over his chest and glared at me. "I am nothing so crass as the media portrayal of my kind."

I bit my lip, but my eyes watered as I tried not to laugh at his indignant expression. "So does that mean you don't live in a bottle?" I blurted the question out before I bent over chortling.

"Why didn't you mention you wanted to see my bedroom?" he said, his voice suddenly right by my ear.

I whirled to face him, my laughter cut short. Before I could retort, vertigo made me close my eyes, and when I opened them, I realized I wasn't in Kansas anymore.

Okay, I'd never been to Kansas, but it was the first thing that popped to mind when I noticed I'd left Simon's white living room. I found myself instead in the polar opposite of that sterile space. Colors, rich colors, ranging from golds, reds, greens, and even blues decorated the circular room strewn with fat, tasseled pillows and one really big, round bed.

Gene, the sly bastard, slipped his arms around my waist and whispered in my ear. "What do you think of my bottle? Wanna fog up the glass?"

"It looks like a set out of a bad seventies porn flick." I shrugged out of his disturbing-to-my-libido embrace and smiled at his chagrined face.

"I'll have you know that I've yet to have a woman

complain about my décor."

"Then you must be a better lover than you look," I said tartly to hide my unease at realizing there was no door out of this place.

*Damn it. Did he make me into a mini-me to fit me in here?*

The thought was a sobering one, and I reluctantly realized I'd better play nice if I wanted him to get me out.

"You truly have no idea about whom you're dealing with," he said musingly.

"Well, excuse me for not receiving the handbook on *Fucked-up Beings that Truly Exist*." I disliked the fact he knew so much and me so little. Not fair. I mean, my siren and werebunny friends never mentioned others, which wasn't entirely their fault. Hell, they were just as clueless as me, having been adopted and raised by human families. How we'd ever managed to find each other was a miracle that I didn't question. I just assumed, given my many years of bad luck, that I was owed a streak of good.

I stumbled as the ground—er glass—beneath my feet shifted. A booming voice echoed inside the glass boudoir. "Gene, get your smoky ass out of there right now and bring Beth with you." Simon punctuated his words with a violent shake that threw me into Gene's arms.

"Don't worry, my pretty," he said with an exaggerated waggle of his brows. "We'll come back and crack the glass with your screams of pleasure once we've gotten to know each other better."

I wanted to refute his claim—after all, I preferred to decide who, where, and when I banged. But I had to admit, his manly assertion, a flirtation not inspired by my succubus powers, excited me. I also wondered if he could live up to his boast. While I'd enjoyed my previous encounters with men, I had yet to find one who really made me want to say, "Wow, you rocked my world."

Then again, given the shaking bottle, didn't that distinction belong to Simon?

Gene wrapped his arms tightly around me, and I clearly felt his erection pressing against my lower back. I closed my eyes as the vertigo from before returned, and when I opened them again, I faced a broad chest. Combined with the body still snugged to my rear, I couldn't help the imp in me from commenting.

"Mmm, my first sandwich. How decadent."

I peered up at Simon as I said the words, expecting a blush. Instead, his eyes glowed with distinct interest, and his hands came to rest on my hips, the thin material of the T-shirt I wore not stopping the heat that his stroking thumb imparted.

"Don't tempt me," he drawled, pulling me hard against an erection that made my eyes widen.

Well, that answered one question. He was giant all over.

Gene purred in my ear, sending a shiver down my spine. "Anytime. Just let us know when you're ready, and that's one wish we can make come true."

Disturbed on so many levels, most of them erotic ones that screamed at me to get naked for some sweaty fun, I moved out from between them. The space separating us didn't help. Looking upon them standing side by side, I had to fight the urge to throw myself back on them and take them up on the offer.

So different looking, yet each tempting in his own way... I needed to leave before I got in too deep—or, should I say, they got into me deliciously deep. But I still had so many questions.

I'd opened my mouth to voice them when music started playing. Given it was an old eighties song titled "Push It," it kind of went with the moment.

"I approve of your choice in songs. But I'll be more intrigued by the act." And there was that heat in my cheeks again as Gene arched a brow and grinned at me devilishly.

Talk about them keeping me off balance. Perhaps I was still fighting off the effects of the drug. For distraction, I followed the singing to my purse, which Simon had apparently rescued along with me. Any moment, I expected them to forbid me from answering, but they allowed me to dig out my pink smartphone from my purse. They didn't do or say a thing when I answered. "Hello."

Claire's voice squealed in my ear. "Where the hell are you? Lana said she went to your room to see if you wanted coffee and your bed hadn't been slept in. Are you okay? Do you need us to rescue you?" How I loved my friends, the first people in what seemed like forever to give a damn about me.

I waited for Claire to take a breath and then hurried to reassure her. "I'm fine. I was waylaid after work, but a Good Samaritan came to my rescue."

"Oh my God. He must have been hot for you to spend the night. You've never done that before." Claire couldn't hide the awe in her tone. She knew me so well, but, in this instance, was wrong.

"It's not like that," I stammered. "Listen, I'll be home in a bit and explain everything."

"Lana says you had better bring some donuts and coffee for giving her a heart attack."

"I will." I hung up on Claire, my overprotective roommate who turned furry and floppy-eared every full moon. Think that was strange? Then you needed to meet my other roommate and BFF, Lana, the siren who was scared of the sea.

"Everything okay?" Simon asked.

"My roommates got freaked when they saw I didn't make it home last night."

"No boyfriend's place to sleep over?" Gene queried.

"Is this you way of asking if I'm single?"

"I'm sorry, was that subtle? Let me correct that. Are you seeing anyone?"

"Not for long she isn't," Simon muttered from where he leaned against the counter.

"I don't think that's any of your business." Look at me, sounding so prim. But I couldn't deny a flare of excitement at their inquiry into my nonexistent dating life. Keeping a boyfriend was hard. Humans couldn't handle my hungers on a regular basis, which made monogamy impossible. Guys couldn't handle that.

"Oh, it is our business. You're our business."

Simon's words held a stark promise that I didn't understand. Peeking at him, I caught him staring at me intently. He might not be an incubus or a vampire, yet that was definitely hunger in his gaze. A hunger for me.

"Now, now, my big friend. No scaring off the sexy cutie." Gene turned to me with a wide smile. "Ignore him. Simon, for all his age, doesn't date much and has little experience wooing a woman."

"In my day, we didn't woo, we took." The big man crossed his arms over his chest.

"Welcome to the modern age where women get to choose," was my tart reply. It hid the warmth that his direct words ignited. "Now, while this has been most interesting, I do have to leave. However, I'd like to meet with you guys again." At their matching sensual smiles, my tummy did a flip. "Get your mind out of the gutter. I want to meet for information."

"But the gutter is so much more fun."

"I prefer a bed," Simon interjected.

"If you'd rather not answer my questions..." I replied.

Gene's grin widened. "Anything you want to know, feel free to ask—or, even better, touch."

As come-on lines went, his was laughably crude, but it worked, dammit. My hand almost reached for him. Bad hand.

Simon shook his head at his friend. "And you say I'm too direct. But in answer to your request, Beth, yes, you may contact us. You're not the only one who is curious. I'll program my number in your phone while you dress."

"Or she could just make a wish," Gene said with a short bow in my direction.

Did that actually work? I might just have to give it a try.

"Speaking of clothes, can I borrow this T-shirt?" I asked, mentally wincing as I imagined the state of my outfit from the previous night—ripped and bloody, and while the wounds on my flesh had healed during my forced nap, I doubted I could say the same for my clothes. Or so I assumed. After all, I hadn't undressed myself.

*I wonder if Simon liked what he saw.*

"I can do better than that old T-shirt," Simon replied with a grin. "In the bathroom, you'll find everything you need. And if I haven't lost my touch, the right size. Just go back to the bedroom and you'll find the ensuite bathroom."

I left the guys and went back to the bedroom, easily finding the clothes on the bathroom vanity. The leggings were a perfect fit, as were the bra, clean panties, and top. He'd even provided a pair of slip-on shoes. All of it was brand spanking new—and white, surprise!—which raised some interesting questions. Had he gone shopping while I was passed out, or had he borrowed them from a female friend? *Maybe they're his girlfriend's.*

An unfamiliar feeling gripped me at the last thought, and I was shocked to realize it was jealousy. A strange reaction for what had been a really odd day, even for someone like me.

Exiting the bedroom, I found the two men facing off, but at my arrival, they turned with smiles that did nothing to hide the tension bristling between them.

"Well, thanks for helping me out." I gathered my purse from the side table and took my phone from Simon's extended hand.

"How are you getting home?" Simon asked.

"Oh, I'll just grab a cab."

"Nonsense," said Gene, stepping around Simon's

restraining arm. "Just tell me where to take you."

"No need to go out of your way. Besides, I need to get donuts and coffee on the way, or my roommates will shoot me."

"Done." Gene snapped his fingers, and a moment later, he held a tray with three steaming Styrofoam cups and a box of donuts.

Cool. And now I was curious. "So, if I tell you I live at 555 Parkview Crescent, you going to snap your fingers and call up a flying rug?"

"Stand here next to me and you'll find out," Gene replied with a wide smile.

Simon snorted. "You are such a showoff."

"Not my fault I'm so awesomely talented."

My turn to make a noise as they bantered back and forth. "You can show me your super genie powers in a second." Because I had one more thing to do before I left. I walked over to Simon and grabbed his shirt to yank him down. He didn't resist, and the scent of him, fresh and brisk, surrounded me. I plastered a kiss on his mouth and whispered, "Thanks for rescuing me."

"Anytime," he rumbled.

What I intended as a small kiss turned into a panty wetter as his big hands swept around to cup my buttocks and lift me so he could thoroughly thank me with his tongue for thanking him.

Talk about electric.

When he set me down, I was a tad wobbly and so freaking horny I wanted to tear his clothes off and ride him until the cows came home. Which would be never because I'd shoot them first so it could last forever.

Yeah, I enjoyed the kiss that much.

But Gene, with a, "Hey, can I join in?" ruined the moment, and I stepped back, stunned at my reaction to a simple kiss.

I so needed to get out of there. Needed to regain some clarity and equilibrium.

"Ready, hot stuff?" At Gene's beckoning fingers, I moved over, casting a last glance at Simon, who steadily regarded me with those intense green eyes.

The genie spread his arms and beckoned for me to stand between them, his outstretched hands still holding the coffee house delights.

"Ala Samantha," he announced, and wiggling his nose, he took me home in the blink of an eye.

As transportation went, I liked it. Fast, free, and I would assume environmentally friendly. Even better, it didn't have same tummy-churning vertigo of the bottle visit.

"Thanks for the ride." I held out my hands for the breakfast treats, and with a resigned sigh, he handed them over.

"I guess this means you're not going to ask me up?" He waggled his brows at me hopefully.

His engaging grin almost did me in, but knowing the inquisition awaiting me upstairs, I resisted. "I doubt you'd enjoy the major girl gab fest. They're going to want all the details. Which reminds me," I said, my eyes widening as I chastised myself for my distraction. "What happened to the vamps that attacked me last night? Should I be looking for a new job?" Or looking to move to a new zip code?

"Vamps?" Gene scoffed. "I doubt you have anything to fear. Simon would have dispatched them before bringing you home. He can't stand the nasty creatures and takes great delight in sending them to the great beyond." Then, as if realizing what he'd said, he stammered. "Well, not that he'd hurt you, of course. You're not really a vamp, even if you— Ah, screw this." He stopped talking and, in a motion too fast for me to track, plastered a hot kiss on me that left my legs shaking and my pussy screaming, "Take me, now." Then, without even a goodbye, Gene, my genie out of his bottle—and I suspected partly out of his mind—left. And silly me, I was sorry to see him go.

I trudged up the stairs to my apartment, the elevator being on the fritz again. I consoled myself with the fact that the exercise meant I could eat more donuts. I'd just made it to the door when it was flung open, and Claire, hands on her hips, stood glaring at me.

"Just where have you been all night, young lady?" she asked sternly. Then she burst into giggles. "Get in here and tell us what happened. And where did you get those wholesome clothes? I've never seen you cover up so much of your body. Is this a new fad?"

I smiled at Claire's babble and walked into the home we'd built ourselves. A collection of mismatched furniture and knickknacks, there was no rhyme or reason to our decorating other than comfort. Lana waved at me from the couch, her feet dipping in a basin of water, probably liberally laced with salt. While tap water helped hydrate her, she needed briny water to truly make her siren side comfortable. Given her irrational fear of the ocean—which I swore I'd keep a secret—she made do with baths, both the full body and foot ones.

We'd learned the hard way that a PMS-ing siren who craved saltwater was nothing to joke about. Although the singing was quite pretty if you managed not to kill yourself while listening to it.

Claire, bouncy and energetic like her werebunny alter ego—and the Energizer one—perched on the couch arm, still babbling.

"So, what happened? Bruno said you left before doing your second set, and he was not happy, by the way. Especially since Bernie skipped off on the job."

Probably because Bernie was dead. But given they didn't mention his body, I had to wonder what had happened to his remains.

I handed out coffee while I debated what to tell them. While we knew each other's secrets, I tended to gloss over the more violent side of my existence. "I'll deal with Bruno when I go in tonight." A smile and stroke of his hand and he'd forgive me anything, a plus from my succubus side. "I had to leave. Some of the guys from the days I was locked up found me at the club." The girls knew all about my past. The only two people I'd ever trusted enough to tell. And I told them mostly so they knew what they were getting into when they hooked up with me.

I'd tried to resist them, tried to stay a loner, but Claire and Lana were determined to be my friends. And I loved them for it. I just hoped my friendship wouldn't kill them.

"Dey fund you?" Lana, mid-chew on a chocolate

donut, choked and spat out a gooey mouthful. "That's not good."

Claire's eyes widened, and her mouth dropped open. "No shit that's not good." The foul word coming from her dainty mouth never failed to make me smile. "What happened?"

"I fought them with a little help." A giant who cleaned their clocks and then rescued me princess style without once taking advantage—the jerk. I omitted the bloody, killing part in my retelling.

"But they're vampires," Lana said, her eyes narrowing. "So who was nuts enough to jump in and help you? Or should I say what?"

"Well, I never did find out what Simon was, although I do guarantee he's not human." That got the girls bouncing in excitement.

"Is he hot?"

"Does he have a brother?"

I laughed at their reaction. "He is drop-dead gorgeous and built like an ox. And while I didn't find out if he had a brother, he does have a friend who's a genie."

Claire squealed, and Lana leaned forward eagerly. "This I need to hear about."

I told them about waking up at Simon's place and meeting Gene. They giggled when they learned about his actual bottle. They sighed over my description of both men and exclaimed when they heard how I'd gotten home with magically produced donuts.

Lana held her donut in front of her and eyed it suspiciously. Shrugging, she took a bite. "Damn, for a magic donut, it sure tastes good."

"So when are you seeing them again?" Claire asked.

Good question. "I don't know. Simon programmed his number in my phone, and Gene jokingly said he'd come if I wished for him. But I don't know. How do I know I can trust them?"

Lana fixed me with a piercing stare. "Oh please. They had ample opportunity to hurt or take advantage of you, and instead, you made it home, unmolested, bearing food and dressed like a nun."

True. Maybe I should have phrased it differently, like *I don't know if I can trust myself around them because since the moment I met them all I want to do is touch them—and lick them, and ride them, and take them up on their offer of a sandwich.* A first for me since I usually fed my succubus need for sexual energy with one partner at a time. I did, after all, still have some warped set of morals.

"I think you should call them and set up a dinner date. It's about time you had a man feed you," Claire said.

A snicker escaped me, given her statement could be taken a few ways.

Poor Claire, she stammered as she added, "I mean the kind of food you put in your mouth." Her voice trailed off as she spoke and I laughed harder. Her cheeks turned a tomato red.

"Get your mind out of the gutter, Beth. And Claire, don't let her screw with you. I think we all understood you meant real food and not the other kind," Lana said dryly.

As my mirth died, I pondered her suggestion. "I will admit I'm curious. They knew what I was right away.

And they implied they'd met others like me before, although, by the sounds of it, they were all killed."

"All the more reason to find out more," urged Lana, the usually levelheaded one. With her encouraging me, I felt more confident that my desire to call was reasonable and not just hormone driven.

"So when are you going to do it?" asked Claire, bouncing again in excitement.

"Don't you mean do them?" I laughed at Claire's red cheeks. For a waitress in a strip joint, she was fairly prudish when it came to sex. Actually, if I were to believe her—and I did—she'd only ever been with one guy, and a piss-poor one at that, judging by the way she shied from relationships. She avoided advances from men, and the times I'd questioned her about her reticence, she claimed she was waiting for the one. I thought it was cute, even though I didn't believe in love myself. Not that I didn't think I could fall in love. I was sure I could. But given my succubus side, any man who ever declared himself—and they were many—did so not because he knew and liked the real me, but because my pheromones made him.

And yet Simon had resisted me. Could it be that love still remained an option for me, albeit with guys who'd missed the boarding call for humanity's ship?

It was nice to have hope.

"I'll call them in a day or two." I didn't want to seem too eager to see them again, even if I missed the guys already. They'd certainly made an impression on me. And when I masturbated in the shower, I didn't imagine one or the other as I stroked my slick flesh. Screw that, I fantasized about them both together with me.

## CHAPTER 4

SIMON PACED his living room as he waited for Gene's return. His emotions and thoughts were in a turmoil, a state far from his usual calm demeanor.

*I have one feisty hybrid to thank for that.* Not that he regretted meeting Beth. How could he when his whole body sang at the sight of her? He couldn't help remembering the sight of her luscious body, which he'd gotten a peek at when he'd cleaned and dressed her while she lay unconscious. She had the curves to tempt a monk. The attitude to withstand adversity. And enough power to handle a man like him.

There weren't many left in the world that could. Yet that wasn't the only reason for his attraction.

Something in him recognized in her a kindred spirit. Someone afraid to trust. Someone hurt by the world. He also recognized that she bore the body of a goddess, with curves and smooth skin that begged for worship.

His cock twitched, and Simon shifted his mind away to more mundane items like, where the hell was Gene?

Irrational jealousy tried to rear its head as an image of Gene seducing Beth—without him—filled his mind. He shook the thought away. He trusted his friend. Gene had earned that trust, and tempting as Beth was, Simon would never let something like interest in a woman destroy it.

Before any other troubling thoughts could hit, Gene returned, a look of bemusement on his face.

"Can you believe she didn't even invite me up?"

His friend sounded incredulous, and Simon chuckled. "She certainly is unique."

"No shit, considering the rest of her kind are dead," Gene replied dryly. Simon winced at the reminder. "Where did you find her?"

Simon's lip curled in amusement. "Would you believe outside a strip joint?"

"You? In a den of debauchery?" Gene's eyes went wide with shock. "Kill me now, for I never thought I'd see the day." Gene flopped onto the couch with his hands clasped to his chest.

Feet shifting uncomfortably, Simon explained. "I was outside, not in, when I found her battling the foul ones."

Gene sat up. "That's right. She mentioned vampires when I dropped her off. I assured her you would have dispatched them."

"Of course I killed them. There's no way I was letting those nasty bloodsuckers run around my town."

"How many did you send back to Hell?" asked Gene.

"A half-dozen."

Gene looked thoughtful. "That many working together? How unusual."

"Funny, but I don't think that's as interesting as the fact that I found a Nephilim." Simon didn't want to talk about the foul ones, even as he struggled to understand his attraction to the hybrid female who, by birth, happened to be half vamp.

"You always did have a knack for sniffing out treasures."

Simon aimed an icy glare at his friend. "She is not an object."

Hands raised in a conciliatory gesture, Gene shook his head. "Sorry. You misunderstood me. No, she's not an object, but you can't deny her value or the beings who will want her, either dead or alive."

At that reminder, Simon growled. Too well he understood the danger to Beth. Too many knew of the prophecy. Too many knew what her blood could achieve.

*She is in grave danger, and I don't even think she knows it.*

For a moment, his iron control wavered. Frost formed on the edges of the furniture around him and crystallized on the concrete walls.

"Calm your beast down," Gene said, not at all alarmed by Simon's uncharacteristic show of power. "She's not in imminent danger, yet. But you and I both know that it's only a matter of time before others, like the vamps, come after her. One only has to be in her presence to sense how special she is. How delicious."

"Then we shall protect her," he stated flatly, including his friend without request.

For the last several hundred years, they'd done most things together—battling the same foes, sharing homes, tag-teaming the ladies. The only thing they hadn't done was each other. There were some lines he wouldn't cross, and thankfully, Gene felt the same way.

Despite their long time together, never before had they both experienced an instant interest in the same woman—make that possessive interest. Simon knew for a fact that Gene didn't show his bottle to casual lovers. The fact that he'd taken Beth into it, and promised she'd come back, said a lot.

As for himself, he couldn't deny his insane attraction to Beth—and the overwhelming need to be with her and protect her. For over two thousand years, he'd walked this earth, and finally, after searching for so long, he was fairly certain he'd found *the one*.

At Gene's chuckle, Simon's attention snapped back to him. A frown creased his brow, as he didn't grasp Gene's sudden mirth. "What's so funny?"

"Well, it just occurred to me that if we're going to keep an eye on Beth, then we're going to have to spend some time at her work. What a hardship, staring at naked ladies shaking their *ass*-ets." Gene leered comically, and Simon's lips twitched.

"I guess it could be worse," Simon admitted grudgingly. "Now, if you're done screwing around, I want you to scout around unobtrusively for information on her. Something doesn't quite add up. How is it she knows so little about herself? And how is it we've never heard rumor of her existence?"

"Yes, the terms babe in the woods and innocent do come to mind. I'll see what I can discover without tipping our hand. And just so you know, before I returned, I laid a protective web over her building to let us know if anything untoward occurs."

A good idea. Simon grunted in acknowledgement.

"I'll be back in a bit." Gene popped out to do his thing, and Simon pulled out his laptop to do a search of his own.

He scoured databases, both human and not, searching for anything that stood out. Other than an increase in vamp sightings and kills starting a few years back, nothing untoward appeared.

After a few hours of fruitless search, he gave up. He needed more info, and for that, he'd need to spend more time with Beth.

What a hardship or, should he say, hard-cock.

## CHAPTER 5

THE MOMENT THEY WALKED IN, I sensed them. It proved kind of distracting, as I was hanging upside down on a pole at the time. I managed to make my unintentional slide down look like part of my routine. However, in my new position, plastered to the stage floor, I couldn't see Gene or Simon. But I knew they were there. I only had to pay attention to my hormones jumping up and down, screaming, "They came!"

Question was, would I come?

As I unwrapped my legs from the pole and rolled to lie on my stomach on the stage, I pushed up with my arms in a hands-and-knees position. I crawled slowly and flicked my head up and down to make my hair arc and flutter in silky strands around my face. I called this my lioness move, guaranteed to make men purr. My doggie position—also a bedroom favorite—allowed me to scan the crowd, and I thanked my enhanced eyesight that allowed me to see past the glare of the lights that spotlighted me on stage.

The guys sat at the bar, and I might have preened to note they watched me and saw me glancing. Simon inclined his head in my direction as our gazes touched. Gene just tossed me a wide grin, along with a thumbs-up gesture.

Despite what I was, all my experience, all my cynicism when it came to men, I couldn't help the flush of heat—a molten, wet desire—from flooding my senses.

*They came for me.* The idea made me quite giddy and aroused. Who could forget their sensual promise of a threesome?

I dry humped the stage in time to the music, my hips rotating sensually in rhythm with my building delight over seeing my new friends again. My excitement radiated outwards, a cloud of invisible pheromones that touched the patrons of the club, erotically so. Catcalls and bills rained over and around me. I didn't bother picking them up. Bruno had an employee to take care of the tips we got for our performances so that his dancers didn't have to scramble all over the stage like crazed magpies. With one last flick of my hair, I rolled to my feet and, with an exaggerated wiggle, walked off the stage.

I exited through the rear curtain and made my way to the dressing room, where I shrugged a see-through, lace babydoll over my skimpy bikini—think teensy, tiny triangles held on by string. I ran a brush through my snarled locks, cursing when the bristles caught.

As I found myself impatiently rushing, I stopped. *Slow down. Breathe deep.* Eagerness to see and talk to Simon and Gene again was no excuse for my actions. A certain amount of decorum had to be shown. Playing hard to get wasn't something I usually indulged in, yet, with these two, I didn't want to rush. Not when I had so many questions, starting with what had brought them by. Please. False modesty did not become me. I chided myself for my coyness. I knew why they were here. To see me.

Confidence restored, I finished brushing my hair and freshened my makeup. I killed fifteen minutes before I finally exited into the club—a girl should never appear too anxious. My iron will kept me from skipping over to them like an eager puppy with her tongue lolling—but my anticipation was still apparent in the damp crotch of my panties.

Refusing to give in to my hormones—even as anticipation increased my level of arousal—I worked the room, speaking to my regular admirers and accepting with smiles their bills stuffed into my bra. I rewarded them with light touches across their cheeks or hands that fed me their desire while making their eyes glaze over in pleasure.

Thus, did I slowly make my way to the bar where, with a nonchalance I didn't feel, I greeted the guys with a simple, "Hi."

Simon chuckled, his low rumble vibrating through me with more effect than the bass of the music blasting. "Nice show."

"I think I've found my new hangout spot. And, might I say, I look forward to receiving a private performance." Gene, the irreverent one, grinned at me devilishly.

"Behave." Simon elbowed Gene, who grunted but continued to smile with twinkling eyes.

Odd, with any other man, I would have probably become offended. Gene was so brazen and cocky, but I liked it, just like I enjoyed Simon's more subtle admiration. The reason, I realized, was simple. I was the one causing the reaction, not my abnormal side, and under their obvious admiration, I bloomed. As did my desire.

"What brings you guys slumming?" I asked, perching myself on a stool between them, the short skirt of my lace cover-up stopping just short of my crotch.

"Just out for a drink," Gene replied with a blasé smile.

"We wanted to see you," admitted Simon with an honesty that shocked and pleased me.

"I'm glad you came." I truly was. In truth, I hadn't stopped thinking of them, and I'd fought the urge to call them all day.

"When are you finished?" Simon asked. "Can we take you to dinner?"

"Ah yes, dinner. We're so very hungry," Gene said with a wink and a leer that had me laughing.

Once again, Simon glared at his friend, and I grabbed his closed fist between my two hands—the man was freaking huge! "It's okay, Simon. Given my profession, I get the innuendos a lot. I've also discovered the ones with the biggest mouths usually have the smallest dicks." I uttered this with a mischievous smile at Gene. My sly rebuke didn't cause him to blush or get angry.

Instead, he laughed. "I think anyone compared to my giant friend would seem inadequate. But I have other skills."

"He does, and not all of them are running his mouth."

Simon relaxed his fist and curled his fingers around mine. "Don't worry, what Gene lacks in size next to me, he makes up for in innovation." The subtle innuendo coming from him caught me off guard, but soon we were all laughing, which, I had to admit, was different than my usual experiences with men. Grunting, sweating, and bellows of "Oh my God" tended to be the more usual interactions I had with the opposite sex.

"Listen, I've got another set to do, and then, if you don't mind waiting, we can go for dinner." And then back to Simon's place or Gene's bottle for dessert. My succubus side would be well fed tonight, and if I was lucky, maybe they'd feed my dark side, too. I wondered what drinking genie blood would do to me. Which reminded me, I still didn't know what supernatural caste Simon belonged to. Werewolf? Nah. Not hairy enough. Titan? He certainly had shoulders big enough.

Before I could straight out ask Simon, Claire approached, wearing her waitress costume consisting of a short black and white maid's outfit along with a bunny tail and ears—the irony of it made us laugh like fiends at home. "Hey, Trixi, who're your friends?" she asked with a bright smile and eager eyes.

I introduced Gene and Simon to her while reining in a suddenly jealous side that reared its head with a snarl at the interest in her eyes. She looked them up and down and then, in a mock whisper, said to me, "You're right. They are yummy."

With a mischievous giggle, she hopped away, leaving me facing two grinning men.

"Cute friend," said Gene. My eyes must have turned

green or smoke must have billowed from my ears, or some other noticeable sign, because he quickly added, "If you're into herbivores. Me, I prefer a girl who likes to sink her teeth into me while I sink into her."

Simon simply added, "Your bunny friend doesn't hold a candle to you." Mollified, even if I didn't understand my unreasonable jealousy, I chatted with them about the club for a few sets.

At a signal from the bartender, I made my excuses and went out back to change. For my next number, I pulled on my darker side, and I dressed to match the part. Black latex undies that zipped up the front, tight bustier held on with laces, fishnet stockings, and lethal high heels. A coating of dark makeup with a blood-red lipstick and I was every man's fantasy of a girl gone bad.

I strutted onto the stage to the thumping rhythm of Rihanna's song, "S&M." A hush fell over the room as I started to dance.

My skin tingled, and I had to concentrate on my motions as I found myself self-conscious, knowing Simon and Gene watched me avidly. I went through the motions for my second act in a heightened state that made me breathe hard. Usually, I could run through my routines with my eyes closed while compiling a grocery list, but having Gene and Simon following my every move added an element of sensuality to everything I did.

When I grasped the pole—thick and hard—between my hands, I undulated my hips at it while locking eyes with Simon's burning ones set in a face tight with tension —the sexual kind. I pressed my breasts around the pole, cupping and squeezing them, and Gene's wicked smile tightened my nipples and sent a rush of moisture to my cleft.

As I undulated, I skimmed my hands down over my body and closed my eyes, momentarily forgetting I was onstage. I danced faster, my motions erotic, my mood even more so. Gasps and sighs came to me faintly, even with the booming music. Flicking my eyes open, I almost stumbled when I saw the front row—my fervent perverts —panting with glazed eyes, their hands hidden under the table.

I bit my lip as I realized my own sexual interest radiated out to touch the humans in the crowd. Not that they were complaining. Several already wore satisfied grins.

Act complete, I almost ran from the stage. My arousal pulsed within, an almost living entity that hungered. But hungered for more than my usual sexual fare. I struggled to understand what had happened. I didn't have much experience with true arousal. I provoked desire. I didn't suffer from it. When my succubus side required feeding, it made me stalk sex in a very clinical manner, but even when I'd starved that side of myself, I'd never found myself in the grips of lust.

Until now.

My cleft throbbed, and my panties were a wringing, wet write-off. My nipples were puckered so hard I wasn't sure they'd soften without some oral attention. I was tempted to lock myself in a cubicle and stroke the bud between my legs to relieve some of the sexual tension. I abstained. As aroused as I found myself, I enjoyed the sensation, for it meant I wasn't just a monster who fed on sex and lust. I could want and need pleasure, the pleasure that came with touching and fucking, because I was a woman. A woman with needs. It turned out I just needed the right man—make that men —to trigger them.

Going through my clothes in the locker, I lamented the fact that nothing I had stored was appropriate for a dinner out. My least shocking ensemble consisted of a black skirt that barely hid my ass, a ruby red blouse, and ballerina flats—which I used in my college coed routine.

Tucking the blouse into the skirt instead of tying it under my boobs, toning down my makeup and securing my hair into a neat chignon, I managed to look like a high-priced hooker instead of a street one. Shrugging, I gave up my battle with my clothes and hoped I wouldn't suffer the embarrassment of being refused service for being underdressed.

*Maybe I can suggest we pick up Chinese food and head back to their place.*

Having made plans to meet them out in the alley so as to not get delayed by clients looking for lap dances, among other things, I headed out the rear door manned by Bruno, who lamented the fact Bernie had walked off the job and not returned. *Poor Bernie.*

"Nice act tonight," the club manager said, holding open the door for me.

"Who says it's an act?" I replied, blowing him a kiss.

Bruno just shook his head. For a man who managed a strip club, he was pretty straight.

The guys waited for me just outside, and I smiled upon seeing them.

Gene's eyes lit with mischief as he looked me up and

down. "And here I was hoping you'd still be wearing the latex."

"Oh, but I am," I replied impishly.

Simon's eyes flared bright for a moment, and I warmed at his interest. With Gene, I knew where I stood, but with Simon, I had to pay closer attention. Such different personalities, and yet I was drawn to both.

We stepped out of the alley, and I felt like the gooey, creamy filling sandwiched between the two of them. We commenced walking, and to my surprise, Simon's thick fingers found and curled around mine. To say his holding my hand pleased me was a vast understatement. It almost made me want to cry.

Say what you would, there was something about holding hands that was intimate, cozy—it made me feel like a precious thing, and I preened under the glow of his attention. Not to mention, because of my illness, I'd never done the whole dating thing with boys. And since my change into a walking menace to society, I didn't so much date as fuck for food and run.

We'd walked only a few blocks when a dark shadow stepped out from an alley, a hideous creature that I recoiled from—not that I got to see it for long. Simon, who surely had some ancient knight's blood roaring through his veins, tucked me behind him, shielding me with his own body.

I swear the man knew how to press my emotional buttons. If I wasn't careful, the big guy would have me falling for him. *And would that be so bad?*

Gene didn't slack off either as my escort. A ball of flame formed in the palm of his hand, and he tossed the fiery orb back and forth, his casual threat more menacing than words.

I should add his nonchalant threat was totally hot too.

I peered around Simon's large form, shuddering as the vision of Hell before me brought back memories of my incarceration—and my past meeting with the benefactor who'd unwillingly provided the darkness to my DNA.

Taller than my gentle giant, the demon stood before us, a hulking, evil presence, whose oily, murky aura ringed him fatly. If I read his shroud correctly, he was as least as old as Simon, but, judging by the darkness in his colors, nasty.

Bright red eyes stared right at me, the evil promise in them wringing an involuntary shudder. The thing sniffed loudly through two holes in its face, the lack of nose giving it an alien visage. The disgusting creature flicked out a black, ridged tongue to lick the tips of its pointed fangs.

The demon didn't speak so much as it hissed. "Step away from the female. My business lies with her."

An obvious showman, Gene spun his fireball on the tip of a finger, Globetrotter style, and replied in a soft voice, "Consider your business cancelled. The woman is with us."

A rusty chuckle from the evil one saw me clenching Simon's shirt as I tried not to react vocally—screaming didn't seem like a good idea, yet. Super sexy succubus and part vampire I might be, but faced with a creature from Hell—yes, Hades did exist—I was a shivering coward. I still well remembered the words of the captive demon upon our forced meeting.

*Human bitch, know that when I escape, I shall tear open your body and feast on your innards. I shall abuse every orifice in your body and create new ones. I shall...*

Needless to say, the demon the government had captured and used in its experiments wasn't happy they'd donated his DNA to mere humans. When they'd accidentally killed him when testing his reaction to an injection of angelic blood, I'd breathed a sigh of relief because I'd had no doubt the confined one would live up to his promises. But apparently, his death had not been the end.

With a mental shake, I forced myself not to let my mind stray as I paid attention to what happened before me.

"Foolish Ifrit. The abomination cannot be allowed to live."

Wait a second, he was talking about me!

It seemed I wasn't the only one not happy with his words. Simon growled, drawing the attention of the demon. "You will leave the woman alone."

The demon flicked its forked tongue and narrowed its eyes. "You keep interesting company, *is dreki*. And here we thought your kind extinct. My master will be most interested in knowing of your existence. Now, do the smart thing and hand the female over. You wouldn't want to draw the annoyed attention of the one I serve."

"Perhaps it is you and your master who should tread cautiously," Gene replied. "The girl is under our protection. So, if you want her, you'll have to go through me and my friend here first. Somehow, I think the prognosis for your success and continued stain upon the world isn't so good."

The demon looked as baffled as I did. Gene, with his flowery words, had confused the subject. Simon cleared it up with a simple, "Touch her and die."

Some part of me must really be warped because his simple announcement totally made me feel all warm and mushy inside.

The demon gnashed his teeth, and his eyes flared bright, but he stayed his hands—make that big, nasty claws. "Have you forgotten the words engraved on both the walls of Heaven and Hell?"

"Whence walks the one tainted unnaturally with the essence of darkness and light, the world shall tremble and the planes known as Heaven and Hell shall cease to exist out of time. *Hail beautus unus, suus cruor vadum attero fines finium...*" Gene recited some strange passage that started in English and then went all gibberishy.

It made absolutely no sense to me but seemed familiar to them. Just another thing that I didn't know since I'd never gotten my membership card to join the club of Fucked-up Beings.

"She must be destroyed like the rest of her brethren in the great cleansing."

"No." Simon bristled in front of me. "She's different than those tainted creatures. Look at her and see her humanity. She is not like those twisted ones."

The beast hissed and snaked a slimy tongue in my direction. "She is the seed of our destruction, and now that I know her scent, I shall not stop the hunt until she breathes her last."

"Then you've signed your death warrant," said Gene, shaking his head.

Simon didn't reply—he acted. The other night, busy fighting for my life, I'd not watched Simon in action. What a mistake.

If it was possible, he seemed bigger all of a sudden as he charged the nasty demon. His shirt strained around muscles that bunched and rippled. I caught a glimpse of long, almost silvery claws, extending from his fingers, sharp talons that he used to slash at the creature.

My would-be knight and the evil villain battled, their weapon of choice—claws, which they wielded like a many pronged sword. The clicking sound and grunts as they jousted back and forth held me riveted until I noticed Gene standing still.

"What are you doing?" I hissed. "Help him before he gets hurt."

Gene turned to me with a look of surprise. "You don't actually think that thing can hurt him, do you?" He chuckled. "Simon's just toying with him."

I fumed. "I don't care. What if someone calls the cops? Or the slime ball gets a lucky shot?"

"Fine, I'll help, but just so you know, I've had a protective shield around us since the fight started to prevent any humans from observing."

Really? I looked around, saw nothing. A growl brought my attention back to the fight.

With a flurry of slashes and pivots, which at times seemed physically impossible, Simon finally struck a killing blow, one that made the demon's eyes widen as it sank to its knees, black ichor gushing from the fatal wound in its chest.

I rushed over to Simon and hugged him while furtively checking for injury. Thus did I hear the demon's last whispery words—even though I wished I hadn't.

"Protect her if you will for now," it hissed. "But know we will return, for we are Legion, and we will kill her before she destroys us all."

Then the light in the demon's eyes went out, rendering them dark and lifeless. A swirling black mist surrounded the demon and with a gagging, sulphuric stench, the corpse disappeared, taking my false sense of security with him.

Reassured Simon was in one piece, I stepped back from him, and placing my hands on my hips, I glared at both men. "Does someone want to explain to me what the fuck just happened? Why does a demon from Hell want to kill me?"

"The information you are asking for isn't the kind of conversation to be had over dinner. Do you mind if we adjourn somewhere more private?" Gene asked with a creased brow that told me, without words, I wouldn't like what they had to tell me.

My first impulse was to say no, but I needed answers. I also wanted the security and familiarity of home and family. While Claire was still at work, Lana was home and would provide an extra pair of ears. "Fine, we'll go back to my place. I've got hard liquor to soften whatever it is you've got to tell me."

"Huddle up then," Gene ordered. Simon tucked me under his arm, his warm solidity reassuring. Gene grabbed us in a hug, and in a shake of Jeannie's ponytail, we were outside my apartment complex.

They followed me upstairs. I led the way, my arousal slowly seeping back as I walked up the stairs, conscious of my short skirt and the view I knew they were enjoying. What they had to tell me must be serious because Gene didn't crack a single joke.

We walked in to find Lana, with her feet soaking, watching *Jaws*—a favorite of hers. She especially enjoyed grossing us out by saying she'd do the shark if she could ever figure out how to change into her tail. Another siren issue she was dealing with, along with thalassophobia.

Her eyes widened as she took in my two companions. I smirked at her and gestured absently at them. "Lana, meet Simon and Gene. Our dinner plans got waylaid because of a run-in with a demon."

"A what?" Lana's screech followed me into the kitchen where I pulled out a bottle of whiskey and poured myself a shot. I downed the burning liquor before grabbing a few more shot glasses and carrying everything out to the living room.

Simon and Gene sat at opposite ends of one couch with a tempting spot between them just right for me. I bypassed the invitation and sat beside Lana.

I poured everyone a generous dollop of whiskey and raised my glass, saying, "*Salut.*"

My friends followed suit, and we slapped our empty glasses down on the table. Fortified by the alcohol, I spilled the encounter with the demon to Lana, whose eyes grew rounder and rounder.

"Ah shit, Beth. That doesn't sound good."

"We'll protect her," rumbled Simon.

"Excuse me," Lana said, and I almost smiled, knowing they were about to see why it was best to leave annoyed sirens alone. "But first off, you just met Beth, and I have a hard time understanding your motives in wanting to protect her in what is surely a deadly endeavor. Second, you both seem to know an awful lot about what she is and what's going on, which I find pretty freaking suspicious."

"We will explain if you give us a moment," interjected Gene. He shut up, though, when Lana, with a high-pitched hummed note, glared at him.

I snickered. My friend did not like to be interrupted when on a roll.

"And finally, exactly how are two guys supposed to stop the hordes of Hell if what the fiend said was true?" When the boys didn't immediately answer—probably too cowed to reply—she let out a shrill whistle that would have probably caused a school of fish to commit suicide.

Gene winced at the strident sound. "Again, Beth, I must say your friends are interesting. I don't think I've ever met a siren who lived so far from the sea."

Lana blanched, and I hastened to shut him up. "Ixnay on the biggay water thingy," I said in very poor pig Latin. I think the finger drawn across my throat with the accompanying gurgle sound got the point across better, as Gene clamped his lips shut.

The smarter of the pair, Simon said not a word, but I could read the mirth in his eyes. Yeah, my friends were special—not quite hockey helmet special, but close. Was it any wonder I loved them?

"Lana's right. You guys know stuff and need to spill." As queries went, I should have probably been more specific, but there was too damned much I didn't know, so I figured any information was better than nothing at this point.

"Where would you like me to start?" Gene asked. "You heard the prophecy. The demon thinks you might be the one mentioned in it and wants to kill you. What I don't understand is how you don't know about the message. Anyone with an ounce of special in their blood knows of the prophecy."

"Humor me," I said, not willing to get into why I'd missed my membership to the supernatural club. "Why is there such a hoopla about some stupid message? Did it never occur to them that maybe someone was playing a joke—a really mean one?"

Gene appeared shocked at what I thought was a reasonable question. "You're a creature of both light and dark. Even if raised by only one side, you should know the message carved using the words of creation them-selves—a power beyond even the Lords of Light and Dark means serious business."

I squirmed. Their assumption that my state of being came from natural means made me uncomfortable, but exactly how should I explain my creation at the hands of mad scientists? I hedged. "So what if some unknown super dude posted a message? I still don't understand why that demon and his friends want to kill me. And what's this about cleansing others like me?"

"About two thousand years ago, when the words appeared on the walls around Heaven and Hell, there was panic. The forces for good and evil, fearing the end was nigh, set out to destroy those they believed the prophecy spoke of."

"The cleansing?" Lana interjected.

"Exactly," said Gene with a sage nod. "All Nephilim, whose blood by birth contained the seeds of both good and evil, were destroyed, hunted down like the vilest of vermin and eliminated. Once the world and the various realms were cleansed of their presence, a ban on matings between angels and demons was put in effect with the verdict of immediate death if anyone chose to ignore it."

"So I'm a Neflim?" I replied, scrunching up my nose at the awkward name.

"Nephilim," Simon corrected. "How can you be so ignorant of your own history?"

He said it in a wondering tone, but I could read Gene's confusion. The moment of my outing fast approached.

"Well, I was kind of raised by humans," I admitted, releasing a bit of the truth.

"Ah, that would explain a lot. Your mother must have been an angel forcefully seduced by a dark one. Giving you up would have been her only option to let you live. I guess your upbringing explains why you seem so human."

I fidgeted at his mistaken assumption. "Isn't there any other way for me to have gotten my powers?"

Gene frowned at me. "Anything other than birth would be unnatural."

I almost snorted. "Unnatural? That's kind if funny coming from a genie."

"You're hiding something." Simon's rumble drew attention to the fact that I wasn't fooling anyone.

"Leave her alone. She doesn't have to tell you if she doesn't want to." Lana came to my defense.

But, the thing was, if I truly wanted to understand, I'd have to divulge the truth.

The very thought terrified me, but, then again, so did getting sliced and diced by a demon.

I drew in a deep breath and decided the time had come to reveal my dark secret. I just hoped they wouldn't regard me as some kind of Frankenstein creation. Then again, I wouldn't blame them because there were times I cried at what those doctors had done to me.

"What if I wasn't born this way? What if I was created?" I whispered the words, ashamed and afraid of their reaction.

"What do you mean, created?" Simon gazed at me in confusion, but I could see dawning understanding—and horror—on Gene's face. Those looks were quickly followed by pity.

So much for thinking I'd be accepted and find answers to who I was. Even among the freaks, I was an outcast.

Angry at the pill Fate had force fed me, I decided to wipe the pity off their face. "You want to know who I am? What made me into a monster?" I smiled at Simon, and in a nonchalant tone that bordered on sarcastic to hide my anger and bitterness, I told them my tale. "I was born human, and by the age of seven, I was sick, really sick with leukemia. The doctors, as soon as they diagnosed me, didn't give me long to live. They hadn't counted on my mom and dad, though. My mom ended up being a close marrow donor match, and she donated to the point she jeopardized her health. Not that she cared. She just wanted me to survive." I blinked back the tears that always brimmed when I thought of the woman who'd birthed and loved me. I missed her so freaking much, even though she'd died years ago—killed because of her love for me. I continued. "My parents, when science kept failing, turned to religion and prayed almost constantly. But God didn't listen to them. God didn't care. So they went back to science. They stayed abreast of all the latest research, but leukemia is a killer, and by the time I hit sixteen, bald as the day I was born, I'd just about given up the fight to live. And that was when my parents got the offer."

Oh, how I remembered their excitement. "A chance," they'd crowed gleefully, even if that chance was experimental. And free of cost, a golden egg to loving parents who'd given everything they had to pay for my survival.

Gene and Simon watched me with rapt expressions, not interrupting me. Lana, at my side, gripped my hand tightly, already knowing my story. I gave them what they wanted to hear, even as I knew my story would make them turn from me in disgust. The demon had been right. *I am an abomination.*

"They flew us and other families in the same situation in like we were celebrities—first class. Everyone was still so happy at that point. We were taken to a top-secret facility, government owned and operated." I jumped up and stood, pacing in front of the couch as I waved my arms. "Welcome one, welcome all, to building nine, where children are mutated as you wait. Hey, Mom and Dad, have some coffee and cookies while you talk with the other parents. Be blinded by our façade while we inject your precious darlings with a toxic cocktail." I mocked the start of my torture, my mechanism for fighting the tears that threatened to choke me. "But as it turns out, while we were receiving our first doses of the vaccine that would change our lives, our parents went through their own life-changing episode. The institution laced their food with cyanide and killed them all. Not that many of us had time to notice or care. We were too busy dying." I spoke stonily, fighting the screaming despair that remembering brought.

Simon's face registered shock, and I stopped him before he could voice his query. "How could they, you say?" I laughed bitterly. "They thought they were doing something for the greater good. After all, we were sick children, and our parents, unfortunate victims in their narrow-sighted struggle for greatness. They told the public they died in a plane crash to avoid scrutiny, and as far as the world knew, we died with them." What I still didn't understand was, why us? Why sick youngsters? Why weren't our parents experimented on as well? What made us so special? Years later, I still hadn't found the answer.

Frame tense with violent energy, Simon bounded off the couch, and he let out a roar that no human throat could have uttered. I gaped at him, once again wondering just what he was. The demon had called him something, but English was my one and only language.

"What did they inject you with?" Gene asked in a

soft voice, drawing my attention away from the pacing Simon and setting me back on track.

"Ooh, all kinds of good stuff." At Gene's stern look, I sobered up. "The government managed to capture a demon and an angel."

I heard a thump and a crack and turned to see Simon pulling his fist out of the wall—a solid brick wall, which now had a hole of crumbled dust. If they were still talking to me after discovering my dirty secret—and I was beginning to think they would by their reaction—I'd have to find out once and for all just what Simon was.

"According to the doctors, who liked to brag, they performed all kinds of tests on their captured prizes. They were fascinated by their ability to heal and regenerate damage. They tried to inseminate human women with their sperm, but it didn't work."

Gene shook his head. "No, it wouldn't have. Special conditions need to be met for their seed to take root in a human receptacle, and even then, the pregnancies rarely come to fruition."

I made a mental note to ask him more about angels and demons later. It was sure to be an interesting conversation. But first, I needed to finish my tale. "They decided to up the ante and inject humans directly with the genes. They couldn't just start picking people up willy-nilly, so they came up with a fabulous plan to use sick children, to have their own parents volunteer them. Thus did the drug trials start with us as the guinea pigs. There were three groups. Those injected with demonic blood. Those with angelic. And then the ones who got both. Most of their test subjects went into seizures and died. They were the lucky ones."

"Don't say that," Lana cried. "You survived, and you're a great person."

I looked at her stricken face, framed by hair that always had a green tinge, despite all the peroxide we poured on it. "It's true, though. Those of us that survived became monsters, ones that need to prey on humans to live. I can be the most awesome person in the world, but it doesn't make what I do for survival right." I turned from her and resumed my retelling of a story that never fully left my thoughts. "In the first group, only some of the boys survived, but the demon gene turned them into vampires."

Gene shook his head sadly. "Humans can be so foolish. They have sown the seeds of their own destruction. This is not good news. I must ask, what powers did your vampires inherit? I wonder if the splicing of the DNA might have made them weaker than those born to the curse."

I looked at him sharply. Born as vampires? There was so much I needed to learn. Especially if I was to survive, for despite the loss of my humanity, I longed to live. I answered Gene's question. "Keep in mind, my knowledge is from years ago when we were no better than caged animals. The boys might have expanded their powers since. Not your classic Count Draculas, my brothers in the institution became a highly intelligent, extremely powerful, psychically gifted bunch with an unfortunate penchant for human blood."

"That's a species-wide trait," Gene said, nodding

while Simon just stood facing the wall, his forehead touching the brick. "Go on."

"I'll start with the tests the scientists did following the legends. The idiots brought crosses and holy water to work. Forget the Catholic drama, vampires, or at least the lab-created ones, don't care about that shit. They do drink blood, and tests revealed that their special diet is what makes them sensitive to the sun, so they go out only at night. The scientists, fascinated with what they'd created, ran them through live simulations to see what a vampire was truly capable of, and how to best kill them."

Gene dropped his head in his hands and shook. "Oh, that must have made the fledglings happy. Let me guess what worked. A stake in the heart, which I might add, kills pretty much everything, along with decapitation, chopping the body to pieces, and fire."

I nodded as he itemized the tortures inflicted upon my departed brothers. "They killed quite a few before they stopped. What fascinated them, though, was their healing rate. Most wounds that would have proved mortal for a human healed quickly. And they could even regenerate limbs after a time. The scientists wanted to harness that ability for humanity."

"And as a vampire ages, his healing abilities increase, as does his imperviousness," said Simon, finally adding to the discussion, his face a stoic mask. But his eyes blazed, and when they looked at me, I felt comforted by the warmth still evident in them.

"That I didn't know. Keep in mind, the ones I knew were only a couple of years old. One interesting thing was the fact that they didn't like to drink the blood of people who imbibed large amounts of garlic or hot spice. Apparently, they taste bad."

"Curry is famous for repelling blood suckers as well. Did they have the power to mesmerize with their gaze?"

"I don't know. They might have, but I never heard of it." I tried to recall if the vamps who'd attacked me outside the club had tried, but in all honestly, I couldn't remember.

Simon moved back to rejoin us, but instead of sitting across from me, he slid onto the couch beside me and, with some titillating manhandling, placed me in his lap. I snuggled into his embrace, a huge relief off my chest as I realized, whether I was an abomination or not, he still liked me.

"Tell us of the second group. The ones injected with the angels' blood," Gene urged.

"Group two, injected with the angel blood, died more than they survived, and in even greater proportion than those who got the demonic stuff. Those that lived through the convulsions became incubi and succubi. They fed off people's emotions and auras. Like the vamps, they were hard to kill, but healed more slowly and could walk in daylight."

"Sexuality is increased in them as the pleasure and intensity of sex allows them to connect with their partner, thus making the feeding more enjoyable and powerful. You said there were fewer of these creations?"

"Maybe a half-dozen if they all escaped when I did."

"And now we come to you, one with both sides, light and dark. How many like you did they create?"

"Ah, yes, the third group, if you count one member as

still making a group. Lucky me, I got dosed with both strains of the DNA. As you both guessed, I've got a vampire side, but I am not affected by sunlight. I heal quickly, and I'm strong. There might be more powers, but I'm not crazy about the blood-lust thing so I don't encourage it."

"You don't need to feed regularly?" Gene asked, leaning forward.

"Maybe once a week or so I've got to pop out the fangs and feed the blood hunger. A few ounces and I'm good." I didn't mention that my victims never even knew what bit them, for I tended to take my blood from an intimate area while feeding my succubus side. Overcome with lust, they never even noticed.

"That's amazing. Natural-born vamps, especially young ones, must feed daily and more than once."

"My brothers could usually go a few days at a time," I said with a shrug. It felt so odd to be talking about this and with people who had answers to some of the things the scientists had wondered.

"What about your succubus needs?"

"Again, I give that part of me a good feed about once a week, but the club makes it easy to supplement in between. The sexual energy is so thick it's like I'm bathing in it, and it keeps me from going all nympho." Lap dances worked especially well because of the light skin-to-skin contact.

"Amazing," Gene said.

Simon's response was to tighten his arms around me. His hug reassured me, but even more awesome—to me at least—was the fact that my science experiment existence hadn't made him run. On the contrary, evidence of his interest poked at my backside insistently.

"I don't know if I'd call it amazing. I mean, I'm thankful that they wiped my leukemia out, but I can never forgive them for taking my parents away and taking my humanity." Although, had they given me the choice, I admit I would have taken life at any cost. And honestly, once I'd escaped, life had ended up not sucking too bad, even if I sucked people.

"So how did you escape?"

"They underestimated us." At the remembrance, I grinned, a feral smile that didn't make Gene flinch. "My brothers destroyed our creators and set the place on fire." The compound was a leveled wasteland of debris, which I was thankful for. I hoped the records of the experiments and our existence were wiped in the conflagration. It was enough I had the Legion of Hell possibly after me. I didn't need the government, too. "In the confusion, I escaped and ran. Eventually, I stopped running and found work that appealed to my succubus needs."

"And met other freaks who let her know she wasn't alone," Lana piped in, squeezing my hand.

I smiled at her. "You're not a freak. You're just different, like me."

Lana grinned back and gave a happy trill. "So knowing she's an experiment, does it make her more or less in danger from the demons?"

A frown creased Gene's brow as he spread his hands and shrugged. "Yes and no. And it's not just the demons who might come after her. Heaven's angels may very well decide to eliminate her, too."

"I thought God's rule was thou shall not kill," I grumbled.

"Humans," Gene corrected. "Anything else is fair game. And keep in mind that the position of God and Devil are elected ones. The rules change depending on who's in power. But don't lose hope. Not everyone believes the etching means an end of everything. There is a group who believes the words signal a new beginning, one where the division between Heaven and Hell is removed and the lines drawn between good and evil scuffed."

I frowned. "Um, is it me or does opening Hell up sound like a bad idea?"

Gene grinned. "Maybe, but we won't know until it happens, will we?"

I wanted to growl at him for being so nonchalant, but I couldn't maintain my scowl. How could I when I'd divulged my dirty secret and not scared them away?

Gene stood. "You've given us much to ponder on. I need to report what you've told me to those who would see you live. You should be safe. Demons, like vampires, are bound to public places or locations they've been invited to. So be sure to not allow anyone to enter whom you don't already know."

"What about angels?"

Simon rumbled behind me. "By killing the demon, we have hopefully eliminated the threat of your discovery. And even if the demons do know, they're not exactly on talking terms with the Army of Light."

"And might I add," said Gene with his characteristic mischievous smile, "that the angels never do anything

73

fast. Too many committees and votes compared to Hell's method, which is do it now or die."

Stupid me, even with this reassurance, I didn't want them to leave. Simon, as if sensing my sadness, squeezed me and whispered in my ear—the loud purr of a lion. "Wear something pretty and be ready for dinner at eight tomorrow. If you need me before that, call. I will come to you if you need me."

I warmed at his words, a reassurance Gene reinforced. "If you're frightened, or need me, make a wish, and I'll come. Fear not, sweet one, we shall keep you safe, even against the Legion. Oh, and wear heels for dinner tomorrow. I have a fetish for sexy feet." He winked at me, and I couldn't help a warm shiver because I read his unspoken intention in his eyes. Me, nude, on my back, my heeled feet up around his neck as he slammed into me.

Sounded like fun. Lots and lots of fun.

Heat and moisture pooled between my thighs, a pleasurable sensation that increased when first Simon then Gene kissed me thoroughly goodbye. Then, like a whirlwind, they left, and with them gone, the silence was deafening.

"Looks like someone is going to get her clock cleaned." Lana cackled.

*More than once if I'm lucky*, I thought with a smile.

## CHAPTER 6

GENE POPPED them back to Simon's place before letting out a string of curses that would have made a pit demon blanch.

"Un-fucking-believable. The humans experimented on her. A mere child!"

Simon calmly went about making them a coffee, reinforced with liquor. The ratio? A tablespoon of coffee to a mug full of whiskey.

"Sons of bitches. If they weren't already dead, I'd stake them out in the desert, pour honey on them, and then call some fire ants." Gene paused in his rant to glare at him. "Why the fuck are you so bloody calm? I got the impression from the fist mark you left at her place that you were pissed."

"I was," replied Simon, squirting a generous dollop of whipped cream onto the drinks. "I am, but I've also had time to realize that, if they hadn't experimented on her, she would have died. While I regret the pain she suffered, she at least lives." His eyes rose to meet Gene's, whose shoulders slumped.

"I hadn't thought of that. And truly, I have no problem with what she is. I am as drawn to her as you are, but keeping her existence secret isn't going to be easy."

"Why, because some random demon came across her?"

Gene shook his head. "No, because the vampires who were created from the same gene as her know of her existence."

"I killed them," Simon stubbornly stated.

"Not all of them. So long as any of them are alive, along with the angelic creations, she is in danger of discovery. Fuck, for all we know, the vampires have already hooked up with a demon and relayed that information."

"Only one way to find out," said Simon, and at Gene's narrowed gaze, his face twisted into a chilling grin. "We find them and question them before we kill them all."

"And if the Legion already knows of her existence?"

Simon smacked his fist into his open palm, the loud sound bringing a dangerous glint to Gene's eyes. "Then we help her fulfill her destiny."

## CHAPTER 7

Troubled for so many reasons, it took me some time to fall asleep, and not just because of the demon who seemed to think the fact that I lived spelled an end to the world. The guys, and my reaction to them, preyed on me.

Why did I feel such a connection to them? It went beyond my wanting to jump them and ride them like an out-of-control cowgirl. I simply liked—no, make that loved—being around them. I loved the way Simon treated me like a fragile princess. The way he thought I needed a hug. I loved that Gene didn't just drool over me. He joked with me like I was his friend.

After my experience in the compound with my brothers, I'd shied from friendships with men. I hated that they all looked at me with lusty eyes, never seeing me, the real person—albeit specially endowed with superpowers.

I had the same problem with human women,

although not to the same extent as men. With human men, all their actions and conversation with me seemed geared toward one thing—getting my pants off. In the past, that had suited me just fine. After all, my mother always taught me to not play with my food.

With Simon and Gene, the sexual attraction was definitely there, along with the innuendos, but it went further than that. They saw me for who I was, not just a sexy succubus. They could have taken advantage of me at any time as well, and yet, they'd acted like perfect gentlemen, even though I sensed their raging desire. They talked to me and listened without staring at my boobs, which was disconcerting. I wasn't used to men looking me in the eyes. I wondered how intense gazing into their eyes at the moment of climax would affect me.

All this musing, though, wasn't getting me ready. I gnawed my lips as I realized something else.

I was nervous.

This was, after all, my first real date. Sure, I'd had guys take me home to see their ceilings, and I'd visited plenty of backseats, but all those encounters had resulted from me siccing my power on the male in question.

Dinner in a nice restaurant where I was expected to keep my panties on while the eating happened, how new and different. The jury remained out on whether I liked it. If I truly wanted to be honest with myself—the horror! —then I needed to also admit the upcoming evening scared the hell out of me.

What if we enjoyed a great dinner and then returned to their place for some amazing sex, and tomorrow, they didn't call, and I went back to being alone? A part of me was terrified that, once they'd conquered my panties, I'd end up ditched at the curb with a broken heart. Stupid me, when did I allow myself to care?

The problem with having in-depth, heart-to-heart conversations with myself? I never liked my own answers.

I finished dressing and headed out to the living room and my waiting panel of roommates, ready to judge me.

"How do I look?" I asked as I smoothed down the skirt of the black cocktail dress I'd bought for the occasion. I'd discovered upon browsing my closet that nothing would do. These men offered me a fresh start. A true chance at something real. I didn't want to wear my usual slutty clothes. This called for something new. That something new was a dress that actually went to my knee. While it hugged my curves, it was far from skintight. It did, however, dip really low in the back, making a bra useless, so it had some redeeming slutty qualities.

"You look fabulous, and you know it," said Lana, taking the sea conch from her ear for a moment. On land, we had cell phones. Under the sea, they used conchs and seashells. Go figure. She'd gotten her hand on one a few years back via the sea market—the ocean version of the black one. While she wouldn't step foot on a beach, she had made some friends and liked to talk.

"Are you sure I look all right? I feel so-so—"

"Dressed?"

Lana totally deserved my mock glare. "I was going to say so proper. What if they don't like it? What if they prefer my usual short skirt and halter top?"

Claire giggled. "I never thought I'd see the day you

were worried about attracting a man, or should I say men?"

I made a face at her. "I'm more worried about looking too hookerish and not being allowed in the restaurant to eat."

They reassured me that I looked elegant, not high-priced. I knew my friends were right—I looked great. On the outside at least, I looked sleek and sophisticated, but under the skirt, I wore a skimpy G-string and my pussy was clean shaven—for their pleasure.

And mine. Tonight was the night.

All my soul searching and disturbing conclusions still led back to one key point. I had been given a second chance at life and, mutant hybrid or not, possible means to the end of the world or not, I'd live life to the fullest and worry about the consequences later. And that motto meant grabbing the boys by their horns—with a firm grasp—and taking what they offered—naked and enthusiastically.

I also had a plan to take care of my ex-brothers, kind of. But I'd need help, and I knew just the two guys to give it to me—and not just in a carnal sense.

A knock sounded, and I jumped, to the amusement of my friends.

Lana started crooning, a certain "Like a Virgin" song.

When my middle finger failed to stop it, I glared at her as I went to answer the door. Upon opening it, I found myself assailed by a jungle. Okay, not a real one, but the wild tangle of blooms thrust at me certainly must have set back the rainforests quite a bit.

Startled—my first bouquet of flowers, sniff.

"These are for you." Simon's voice was hidden behind the dense foliage.

"Thank you." I hid my surprise and delight by grabbing the supersized bouquet and heading to the kitchen to find something to put them in. An acre of land came to mind, but by splitting the floral arrangement into every large container I could find, I managed to find the time to calm my shaking hands. Like a virgin indeed, I snickered to myself.

Chiding myself for being a ninny, I took a deep breath and headed back out to the living room, where I could hear the rumble of voices.

I stopped dead at the sight of Gene and Simon. I didn't have a choice because I needed to clamp my thighs tight to stop the shudder that went through me. Yes, I got instantly aroused, but who could blame me when they looked so yummy?

I wasn't the only one who'd taken care with her wardrobe. The guys looked splendid dressed in matching suits with—gasp—ties. The wicked vixen in me could already imagine those naughty neck nooses lashed around my wrists as I writhed beneath their sensual touch.

With those kinds of thoughts already rampaging through my mind, however, would I make it through dinner?

Their eyes shone with admiration, and their smiles reflected their happiness at seeing me. Simon approached me first and grasped my hand in his big paw. He lifted my trembling hand and, twisting it slightly, placed a hot kiss on the inside of my wrist. I shuddered, and I would have slumped into a boneless puddle at his feet had he not released my arm to slide his own around my waist, supporting me. I was in so much trouble if such a simple gesture had me losing all my motor skills.

Gene approached me next and leaned in, kissing me softly on both cheeks, European style. The subtle aroma of his cologne tickled my senses. His whispered, "It felt like an eternity waiting for this moment." Corny, and yet it was enough to almost make me close my eyes and swoon.

A snort from Lana with a, "Get a room," revived me a bit, as did the unexpected blush that crept up my face.

Claire sighed. "Oh, I can't wait to find a man who makes me feel like that."

"You'll be meeting him sooner than you think," Gene said to her cryptically before bowing in their direction. "Ladies, if you'll excuse us, we have reservations."

And just like that, I was whisked away. Instead of using a limo, Gene hugged Simon and me, and with a nod of his head, we were elsewhere.

We stood in the vestibule of a swanky joint, the polished wood, thick carpeting, and gold accents screaming old school. I heard the sound of a throat being cleared and turned to see the maître d'. And that's when I realized, fancy place or not, I doubted Chef Ramsey had ever heard of this place. The lizard man in the suit with the bowtie inclined his head at us, and I bit my lip so as to not rudely blurt out a very unladylike, "What the fuck?"

The guys saw nothing amiss with our host, so I took their cue and pretended a nonchalance I didn't feel.

"We have reservations." Simon tugged me forward to stand before the podium, upon which sat a thick book, the pages uneven and yellowed, with, of all things, an ink well and quill alongside it.

"Your name?" asked the lizard thing with what I could have sworn was a sneer.

I'm not sure what Simon did behind me, but the maître d' recoiled and adopted a more servile expression. "Of course, sir. Sorry for not recognizing you. Please, follow me."

We followed the lizard man, who, to my amusement, had a tail sticking out of the back of his pants. We passed dozens of tables, partially hidden in shadows, but not dark enough for me to not realize that most of the patrons weren't descended from Adam and Eve.

I recognized some species—like the dwarves with their big beards and short, stocky stature. There were some fairies with gossamer wings whose sizes ranged from Thumbelina to human-sized. The one-eyed scary dude was, if I remembered my mythology correctly, a Cyclops. And at the sight of a bright blue demon, I clutched tightly at Simon's arm.

He followed my gaze and patted my hand reassuringly. "Don't worry. We'll explain things in a second."

His words made my eyes widen because I immediately grasped the implication. "You're using me as bait," I hissed. I'd actually contemplated doing that, and it was part of the plan I'd meant to broach over dinner. It annoyed me that they'd acted without consulting me first, never mind I'd had the same thought. I didn't take kindly to them making decisions for me. Especially ones that affected my life—and how long I would get to enjoy it.

"Bait is so harsh, don't you think? I prefer the term 'showing you off,'" Gene replied as we arrived at our table. With a flourish, he pulled out a chair for me.

Some women would have turned on their heel and walked out. But to leave meant foregoing answers or forging ahead alone. Could I trust they had a plan and, more importantly, my best interest at heart?

Head held high, I sat, and my dates took positions on either side of me. For a moment, I stared at the dark damask tablecloth, the only safe place to look, as I feared what my roving gaze would see.

The back of my neck prickled as I imagined myself the object of everyone's stare. I drummed my nails on the table, stopping only when Simon captured it. But even the hand holding couldn't ease my tension. With a terseness that wouldn't allow me to relax, I said, "Explain."

To my surprise, Simon answered instead of smooth-talking Gene. "After our encounter with the demon, and then your admission of your past, it originally occurred to us to keep you hidden. To secret you away somewhere safe."

"You wanted to make me a prisoner?"

"Never." Simon raised my hand to his lips and brushed his lips across it. No matter my irritation, my body betrayed me with a shudder. "We would have kept you in the lap of luxury while we hunted down the vamps you were created with. We planned to destroy them before they could tell anyone of your secret."

"You speak as if the plan changed?" A pity because I rather approved of eliminating those who wanted to harm me.

"It did because, as Gene pointed out, we couldn't be sure none of them had already slipped and told somebody. What if we missed one? There are many who'd find your existence a tasty tidbit to sell."

"So no killing?"

A rumble shook him as he chuckled softly. "Never fear, the plan is still to kill them, but we're also after some bigger prizes."

"Bigger than my vampire brethren? Like who?"

Gene leaned close, his words tickling across my earlobe. "We want those who'd use that information."

Understanding widened my eyes. "Are you out of your freaking mind?" I hissed through clenched teeth. "What part of hordes of demons and angels gunning for me did you not get?"

It was Gene's turn to chuckle. "Calm down. We won't let you get hurt. We would never allow you to come to harm. Have a little faith in us. A little faith in the world."

"Hard to have faith when the world seems determined to kill you." Yeah, there might have been a touch of bitterness in there.

"It is said what does not kill us makes us stronger."

I peeked at Simon and snorted. "In your case, I guess people didn't like you a lot."

It took him only a moment to grasp the jest, and when he did, he laughed, a big booming sound that turned more than one gaze our way. But, oddly enough, seated between them, I wasn't scared. Nor plotting flight.

Could they truly have a way of getting me out of this prophecy mess?

"You probably don't know this, but you have more allies than you realize. Angels and demons are just two sects who would be content with things staying the same. Remember how I told you there was a movement to let the prophecy come true?"

I nodded.

"I talked to some of my contacts about you, and you'll be pleased to know that they'll protect you."

"Gee," I said with a sarcastic lilt while rolling my eyes, "I feel so much better now. I get to trust strangers with my life."

Simon's immense hand squeezed mine. "Your life is safe. They'll have to go through me or Gene first, and as you noted, I'm not this big for nothing. I can handle whatever they throw at you."

I would have retorted, but at that moment, the most beautiful woman in the world—who happened to have wings of translucent gold—approached our table. Instinct drove me to my feet as I subconsciously understood that staying seated in front of her would be disrespectful. There was something majestic about the otherworldly woman, something that demanded respect.

Eyes of gold gazed upon me, and I shivered, sensing the power in her stare. I fought the urge to kneel before her, and after a few moments of silence, she spoke, her voice lilting and musical. "Finally, the one foretold has arrived. Welcome, dear one. Should you require aid in your quest, you may call upon me."

Say what? I looked on her blankly. "Um, thanks." While I appreciated her offer, I hadn't the slightest clue who she was.

"Queen Mab, you do us great honor," said Gene, who'd also stood, along with Simon.

"A token has already been sent to your court in thanks for your kindly gesture," rumbled Simon.

The queen's eyes glowed, and her lips curved into a smile that held a touch of avarice. "A treasure from you fabled hoard. I am spoiled. And might I say how glad I am to see you. I knew the rumors of your demise had to be false." The golden gaze flicked to me. "Congratulations on your choice."

With an incline of her head, the queen departed, leaving behind a scent of sunshine—and a host of questions. We all sat back down just as a waiter—an actual monkey dressed in a suit—arrived with wine glasses. I waited until he'd poured us all a brimming glass full and left before I spoke.

"Who the hell was that woman?"

"That, my dear girl, was Queen Mab, ruler of the fey. To have her on your side is no small feat."

"Is that what she was saying? But why? Why would she offer to help? She doesn't even know me." A frown knit my brow.

"I told you not everyone believes the prophecy means an end to all. There are some tired of the games Heaven and Hell play."

"Fine, so the fairies are on my side, but what was this

87

about a treasure?" I turned my gaze on Simon, my enigma. "Why is it everyone who meets you acts like you're some kind of god? Just what are you, and why do they think you're so scary?"

"You don't think I'm scary?" he replied, sidestepping my question with a grin.

"No, but if I don't get a straight answer, you're going to discover how scary I can be." I had my own theories, as did my roommates—and twenty bucks riding on the answer.

"I'm an ice dragon."

I blinked. I looked him up and down. Then sighed.

"What? You asked for the truth," he said, spreading his hands.

Gene chuckled. "Perhaps you should go outside and show her your magnificent alter ego."

"No, I believe him. I just can't believe how wrong I was."

"What did you think I was?"

I squirmed. "Well, I had a few theories. I had you narrowed down to a Titan—"

"Much too small," replied Gene.

"Or an incubus."

"Not pretty enough," snorted Gene while Simon, looking astonished, blushed.

"Claire thought you were a shapeshifting polar bear, and Lana actually thought you were some kind of deity like Poseidon."

Simon grinned. "She thought I was a god? Don't worry, after tonight, I'll prove to you that I am and much more."

It was my turn to blush as his words spread heat through me. But I wasn't quite done with them yet. I took a sip of the wine and almost choked. "What the heck is this?" I asked as my eyes watered.

"Dragon ice wine, a potent concoction for the uninitiated," Gene said dryly.

"I like it," said Simon stubbornly, swigging it.

"Fine, whatever." I pushed the glass aside and went for the crystal goblet of water, which certainly hadn't come from any municipal tap. "Now, before we get off topic, there are a few more things we need to talk about. Like, how is this dinner going to lead us to my vampire brothers?"

"Oh, someone here will blab," stated Gene with assurance. "And if the vamps don't make a move, then we'll try something bolder. But I'm pretty sure someone will sell them the info. After all, only the blood of a Nephilim can allow a night stalker to walk in daylight."

"Whoa, stop right there. First of all, I looked up that Nephilim thing, and Wiki says they're the result of an angel banging a human."

Gene made a buzzer noise. "Wrong. Angels who mate successfully with humans make incubi and succubi. While demons who mate with humans, without killing them, make vampire babies. Nephilim are a mixture of both angel and demon. Although, you're the first I've heard who started out human."

"Fine, so the Internet was wrong. Now, how come only my blood can let the vamps walk in daylight? What about the fairies? Aren't they like sunshine and stuff? Wouldn't they make a better choice?" The words popped out of my mouth before I could stop them, and I quickly peered around to see if any fairies overheard, but no one seemed to be paying us attention.

"Fairies are pure poison to the dark ones," Simon answered. "No one knows why the blood of the Nephilim is the only thing that allows vampires to walk during the day. In the old days, before the cleansing, Nephilim used to be little more than blood slaves to the vamps."

I shuddered. "Okay, change of topic. Let's say I go along with the plan to be bait. I need to know how to fight."

"From what I saw, you did a fine job on your own," said Simon with a creased brow.

"That was hand-to-hand stuff. I'm talking about learning to use my powers to help me instead of having to use my fists. I mean, I've got the wings and learned to kind of fly, but—"

"You have wings?" interjected Gene, looking surprised.

"Yeah. Why? Don't all Nephilim have them?" I looked back and forth between them and tried to hide my shock when I realized the answer. "I'm a freak," I mumbled, slumping forward to hide my face in my hands.

Big hands tugged at mine, and I lifted my face reluctantly. Simon peered at me with a quirky smile. "I can turn into a huge dragon and blow ice. Not to mention, grow claws, a tail, and cause all objects around me to become layered in frost. Does that make me a freak?"

"No, because that's part of who you are."

"And your wings and whatever other secrets you've acquired are a part of you. So what if you're not like the Nephilim of the past? Think of yourself, instead, as the new and improved model. There's nothing wrong with being different. Take a look around you. You're not alone."

"I've got an idea," Gene announced amidst the seriousness. "We need to give her a name of her own. Since she's not quite a Nephilim but a new class of being, she deserves the chance to name herself as the first of her line."

At first I wanted to tell Gene where he could shove his idea—in a place that light didn't shine—but something about owning who I was actually appealed. But what could I call myself? "You know what, I like it, but how do I decide on a name? I mean, what if there ends up being others like me in the future? I don't want to leave them saddled with a name they hate."

We mulled this together as our monkey server arrived, bearing plates piled high with what looked like a Caesar salad. I'll admit I was disappointed. I kind of expected blue lettuce and some kind of alternate-dimension dressing, but after tasting it, I could at least concede it was the best freaking salad ever.

"Humangon," said Gene all of a sudden.

I wrinkled my nose. "That is horrible."

Simon paused eating long enough to say, "Humaneph."

"Bless you," I said sarcastically. "Come on, can't you think of something that describes me, the sexiest hybrid misfit ever?"

"That's it!" announced Gene.

"What? Sexiest?" I queried.

"Hybrid misfit." Gene clapped his hands. "It's perfect."

I mulled it over, and a lightbulb went off inside my head, the brightness of it making me blink. "You're right, and it won't just be for me. I'm not the only one who doesn't fit in. Look at poor Lana, a siren who can't change into her fishy self or go near the ocean. She could be a misfit, too."

Gene laughed. "And the wood nymph who prefers celibacy. She can be a misfit as well."

"Anyone who's not human and who doesn't want to conform can belong," I said, getting into it. "We'll have T-shirts done up. We'll start a club."

I giggled, joined by the guys, and even though I knew we were the object of stares all around, I found myself not giving as much of a damn. *Misfits aren't meant to conform, and starting with me, I'll forge my own path, thank you very much.* Starting with my seduction of my two dinner partners.

Right after the main course, of course. Even I couldn't resist the mouthwatering aroma of the prime rib placed in front of me, and if the meat wasn't like any bovine stuff I'd eaten before, I ignored it because it was ambrosia in my mouth. And besides, misfits weren't afraid to try new things—say, like, my very first threesome.

Now that we'd tackled the boring stuff, I found myself recapturing the lust from earlier. We made small talk, the conversation and laughter flowing smoothly.

Every so often, Simon's hand would slide under the table and squeeze my thigh—after pushing my skirt up first. The heat of his palm resting on my skin made me shiver. I kept hoping he'd move his hand over and dip a finger into my soaking honey pot, but the big tease would rub me for a moment then move his hand away.

Gene employed a different tactic. He'd cut a prime morsel and then pop it into my mouth—with his fingers. I'd suck them clean, and his eyes would glow. I wondered if anyone would notice if we disappeared under the table for a moment.

Looking at the easy camaraderie between them, I suddenly felt a burning need to know. "How did you guys meet and become friends?"

The boys looked at each other and laughed. At my questioning look, Gene, with a sheepish smile, said, "To understand, first I need to admit that I pissed off a powerful sultan. He didn't take kindly the fact that I'd seduced and ruined all the women in his harem. " At my arched brow, he grinned even wider. "All one-hundred-and-forty-seven of them. He had a Djinn of his own who lived in a brass lamp. Using one of his wishes, he had me cursed and sealed in the bottle I showed you then cast into the ocean."

I leaned forward, rapt. "It's like something out of *The Arabian Nights*."

Simon laughed at Gene's scowl. "Don't remind me of that tale. Who do you think the Djinn in that story was?"

I giggled. "So how long did you end up swimming around in your bottle?"

"Oh, a thousand years or so."

That shut me up and wiped away my smile. "Oh, Gene, how awful."

"Yes, it was," he replied soberly, only to grin again a moment later. "Actually, it ended up just what I needed. I mostly napped during that time, caught up on some reading, and basically relaxed. Until the day a wave tossed me up on the icy shores of the Antarctic, that is, and a covetous dragon stole me and hid me away in his hoard of treasure."

Simon almost choked on the wine he'd just swallowed. "Stole? Ha, you washed up on my beach, and the rule is finder's keepers. Besides, your glass bottle was pretty and went well with my collection."

"You actually have a treasure hoard?" I asked, distracted like a crow by a shiny bauble.

"Oh yes, and if you're a *good girl,* maybe I'll show you," he promised with a wink.

"Hello? We were talking about me," Gene interjected. "And if you want treasure, I can show you things that this here old dragon can only dream of owning."

I giggled as they argued back and forth over who had the most priceless item. Eventually, I waved my hands and declared a draw. "Back to the story. Simon found your bottle and then what? Rubbed it and out you poofed?"

"Ha, I wish. My friend here didn't even realize I was in there for the first hundred years, and trust me, it wasn't for lack of trying."

Simon shrugged. "Just because I hear disembodied voices doesn't mean I reply."

As answers went, his was strange, but his wink led

me to understand he was yanking my leg, although all this banter really made me wish he'd yank something else.

"Eventually, my cold-blooded captor opened the bottle," Gene said with a dramatic sigh.

"I needed a container to store some wine," Simon explained.

"And while we initially clashed—"

"Because I'd chosen to move away from humans and Gene wanted to rejoin them."

"We discovered that we quite enjoyed each other's company, and thus was the greatest friendship in existence born."

Simon rolled his eyes. "Oh, please. He just likes bragging that he's friends with the last ice dragon. And, besides, he wouldn't go away."

That set them off on another friendly squabble that put me in stitches and, with them still taunting my body with fleeting touches, at the same time, revved my desire.

Dinner took forever, or so it seemed to my extremely aware body. When the monkey server asked if we wanted dessert, I almost screamed, "Yes, the cream-filled tube kind," but Gene waved him away.

"I think we can come up with something sweeter and more satisfying at our place," Gene said to me.

My sex watered in agreement. I'm not sure how I managed to stand on legs that wobbled like a newborn colt's. The men bracing me on either side surely helped.

We'd no sooner popped out of the restaurant back to Simon's loft than I lost the battle with my arousal.

I turned into the chest of my friendly giant and tilted

my head just in time for his lips to claim mine. His firm mouth clung to mine, and I snaked my arms around his neck, pressing myself against his solid length. At my back, Gene's body pressed against me, his scorching lips teasing the sensitive skin of my nape.

Oh sweet heat.

Molten desire poured through my body. I was so hot and ready for them. My fingers clenched at the fabric covering the skin I wanted to explore. I tugged and mewled against his mouth. A chuckle in my ear made me shiver.

"Slow down, precious one," Gene said, flicking his tongue against my ear lobe. "We have all night."

With those promising words, I was swept off my feet and carried into a bedroom with the biggest damned bed ever. Simon tossed me onto the snowy white cover, and I bounced with a squeal.

Holding my gaze, Simon stripped off his dinner jacket and loosened his tie. "Hey, Gene," he said over his shoulder to the genie who'd also stripped off his coat. "I think our little hybrid misfit here is a touch impatient."

"Are you thinking what I am?" Gene tugged off his tie and snapped it between his hands.

Simon smiled, and in the blink of an eye, I found my arms pulled over my head and attached to the bedposts with their ties, a fantasy come true. They left my legs free, but still, just knowing I was at their mercy made me freaking wild, and I trembled with anticipation.

"Oops," Gene said with a naughty twinkle in his eyes. "We forgot to remove her dress first."

"I'll take care of that," Simon replied, kneeling on the

bed between my legs. I squeaked as I realized he meant to rip the dress off me.

"I just bought this," I protested.

"I'll buy you dozen to replace it," growled Simon. He'd no sooner spoken than, with a tearing sound, my dress was ripped from my body, leaving me clad only in my G-string. "Perfect," Simon murmured before burying his face between my breasts.

"Um, aren't you guys a little overdressed?" I panted as he worked his mouth over to one of my taut nipples. Then I didn't really care because he took my aching peak in his mouth and sucked. I cried out at the intense sensation, my body arching up to strike his.

"She's right," rumbled Simon, pulling his mouth from my bud. I pulled at my bonds, wanting to grab his head and put it back where it belonged—pleasuring me.

But I changed my mind when I saw both guys move to stand at the foot of the bed and start stripping. The shirts came off, the popping of flying buttons revealing two magnificent chests. Simon's was wide and covered in slabs of muscle. He also appeared hairless and bore pale skin that rivaled that of white marble. I wanted to run my hands over his smooth flesh down his wide chest to his tapered waist, then bump over his splendid abs as I explored the tantalizing vee that disappeared into his slacks.

But he wasn't the only body that deserved exploration. My genie had a treasure for me to discover too. Gene possessed a slimmer build, but he was very well toned with an even caramel tan and flat nipples pierced by golden rings.

With such delectable options, I couldn't decide which torso I wanted to explore first.

Not that they gave me a choice—how exciting. Without a word, they each took up a position on either side of me. Like synchronized lovers, they each latched onto a nipple, their mouths both hot and yet different in their technique.

Under their oral caresses, I grew wild with want, my sex slick with juices and my clit throbbing for attention. As if just thinking of my poor pussy relayed a psychic message, a questing hand slid down my body, wait, make that two hands, one on each side. I parted my legs for them, and while one delved between my soft folds to insert itself into my ready channel, the other found my clit and stroked it.

The intense sensation, along with the mouths sucking at my protruding nipples, was enough to send me over the edge. I climaxed quickly, the quiver of my release clamping my sex around the fingers pumping me. I cried out, my lower body bucking.

"Good girl," whispered Simon, who'd slid his mouth up to my neck. "Now kiss me." I turned my face sideways and found his mouth. His slick tongue parted my lips and found mine for a wet duel.

Engrossed in our embrace, I lost track of Gene, but remembered him real quick when a hot tongue darted out to flick against my clit. I bit Simon's lip in surprise, and he grunted, but he didn't pull away. The metallic flavor of blood hit my taste buds, and my dark side tried to rouse. Already battling my succubus side—which fought to feed at this buffet of sensual delights—I moaned and pulled my mouth away.

"Feed from me," he whispered, following me. "You will not harm me."

I would have protested, but he pressed his bitten lip against my open mouth. I couldn't resist. I sucked at his pinprick wound. The minute amount wasn't enough for a true feed—delicious and exotic as his blood was—but it quelled my dark side, for the moment.

My succubus side was another matter, though. Gene's mouth worked insistently at my sex, and despite my recent orgasm, I found my arousal building again, tightening my channel. My sexual nature also sensed their torrential desire, and as much as I tried to hold my succubus side on a leash, I could feel my grasp weakening.

Distracted, I stopped responding to Simon's embrace, and he moved away to my belated chagrin. He returned quickly, though, and he straddled my upper chest with his naked body. Startled, I opened my eyes and then opened them wider as I took in the size of the cock jutting from the vee of his thighs.

"Good grief, you're huge." My sex clamped down around Gene's tongue in excitement, and my mouth watered at the thought of tasting Simon.

The tip of his cock pearled a drop of fluid as I stared. I craned my head toward it, but couldn't quite reach. Simon thrust his hips forward, and the tip of his shaft entered my open and waiting mouth. I licked the pre-cum and then sucked at the mushroom cap, trying to get more, for his unique flavor hit my tongue and I craved more.

I looked up to meet Simon's glowing gaze as I slid my lips along the length of his shaft. The cords in his neck tightened as his rod filled my mouth, my teeth grazing him. He was just too big for me to take completely, but I did my best. In my position, bobbing my head was hard, but Simon took care of this by fucking my mouth, his hard prick going deep enough to gag me then withdrawing.

Not to be outdone, Gene finally stopped his oral torture of my pussy, and I felt my pelvis hoisted. The tip of his shaft probed at my wet slit, and I moaned around the rod in my mouth. I wanted him to fuck me so badly. But Gene teased me, rubbing his swollen head against my sensitized nub, making me mewl around Simon's prick. Restrained by ties and bodies, I was at their mercy, and while it frustrated me that I couldn't take what I wanted, it also made me wilder than I ever recalled getting.

After what seemed like an eternity, Gene impaled my sex on his long cock with its curved tip. I grunted at the welcome penetration, my channel squeezing tight and sending jolts of pleasure throughout me. Slowly at first, Gene pumped me, his thrusts matching those of Simon's, still filling my mouth.

It was exciting and different. Trying to concentrate on my oral technique with Simon's cock versus the fucking of my pussy was distracting. One moment, I'd suck energetically, only to lapse when Gene would pound vigorously at my willing flesh, sending me spiraling on the wings of pleasure. Then Simon would remind me of his large presence by probing the back of my throat with his shaft, and off I'd go again, working his thick rod.

A particularly hard series of thrusts, and a new angle, had the tip of Gene's cock finding and striking my G-spot —over and over. The jolts made me forget the shaft in my mouth, and I clamped down, lost in bliss.

Simon hissed, and I loosened my oral grip. I opened my eyes to see his eyes smoky with pleasure.

"Suck," he ordered, even as I felt his blood trickling down my throat. I needed no further urging. My dark side took over and sucked at the inadvertent wound that pumped his life force into me. It fed me and drove my rapture to new heights.

My cheeks hollowed, and I inhaled him, hard and fast. His fingers twisted into my hair, aiding me in pumping his cock down my throat. I felt him tighten before he came in a creamy rush that filled my mouth and spilled out. I wanted to smile with the knowledge I'd made him lose control. Simon withdrew his shaft from my mouth and moved off of me to the side.

Gene's cock still worked me, his body glistening with sweat as he pistoned my channel. He smiled when my eyes caught his, and he increased his pace, sending me into a series of mewling gasps. My pleasure coiled inside me, and without Simon's weight pinning me, I arched my hips, meeting him thrust for thrust. Gene leaned down over me, his muscled arms keeping his full weight off of me.

"Take what you need," he whispered before kissing me. I wasn't going to. After all, my succubus side didn't really need feeding. But when Simon's big fingers pinched my nipples while Gene swirled his cock against my sweet spot, I came hard. In the throes of an orgasm—a nine for sure on the Richter scale—the leash I held over my needs slackened, and I took what Gene offered.

I sucked his tongue into my mouth, and as I tasted him, I opened my other mouth, the esoteric one that fed on pleasure and emotions. The rush of power that flooded into me threw my body into another climax before I'd completed the first. I shook with the force of it, and still Gene poured himself into me, his body pounding away until finally, with a cry I heard with my mind and not my ears, he came, a hot torrent that filled me in more ways than one.

Even half conscious, I knew to pull away before I drained him too far. I tore my mouth from his, panting. Gene collapsed on the bed beside me, his breathing ragged. I stared at the ceiling as I tried to regain my breath, my being radiating satiation and power.

"Wow," I managed to say.

Thick fingers wrapped around mine, and I turned my head to smile at Simon, who lay propped beside me on one arm. "And that's just the beginning," he promised with a grin.

My hand was grabbed on my other side, and I swiveled my head to see Gene with a beatific look on his face. "Screw hybrid misfit. I think we should call her awesome."

I blushed at his praise. Somehow coming from a guy who had superpowers and lived longer than I cared to think about—and fucked an entire harem on his own—it said a lot. I hoped. Or did he say that to all the girls? *Nah, I know I'm good. And, I'll admit, that was a personal best for me.*

"Still hungry?" rumbled Simon.

I frowned. "You know, you guys didn't have to feed me. I can fend for myself."

"Not anymore," Simon growled, followed by Gene with, "There's no need."

"What do you mean?" I asked. Sometimes I could be clueless, and while I had an inkling of what they meant, I needed to hear it said.

"From now on, if you need to feed, you use us."

A part of me bristled at his caveman answer. *Who made him the boss of me?*

Gene smoothed it over with, "Having grown quite attached to you, it would please us if you would turn to us if you need feeding, as we cannot be sure of our jealous reaction should you choose to feed off another."

"Oh." They liked me? I warmed up, not just my desire, but my heart, too. "What if it's an emergency?" I queried.

"Emergencies are fine, but if we have a say, we'll never be too far from your side."

I frowned. "I'm not moving in."

"Yet," said Simon with a smile.

I knew I should have probably been a little annoyed at their gently put command, but I'd never had a boyfriend before, and now it looked like I had two, and while they'd share with each other apparently, nobody else could join in. It was kind of hot.

"Now, on a different note, didn't someone say something about pleasuring me all night?" I queried with a naughty grin.

I laughed when they pounced on me with eager hands and mouths. And true to their word, I spent a blissful night, and I didn't fall asleep until dawn touched the sky, smooshed between my lovers, clasped, to my delight, in their arms.

## CHAPTER 8

I woke to find Simon gone and Gene still wrapped around me. I ran my fingers over his bald crown, blushing when I remembered what he'd done with that shining pate the night before.

Who'd have thought it would be so arousing?

Gene stirred and stretched with a yawn. "Morning, gorgeous," he said, cracking open an eye.

"Hey you." I grinned at him, much too pleased with myself this fine morning.

"How's the most beautiful hybrid misfit in the world?" asked Simon, coming in with a tray laden with food.

"Starving." I bounced on the edible offering with a voracious appetite, for while they'd fed my esoteric side, my human tummy still required nourishment.

"That's a girl. Eat up. You're going to need the energy," Simon said with a wink.

I sat up straighter, and pushed out my chest with a

coy smile. "I've got tons of energy anytime you're ready, baby," I cooed.

"Great. Grab a shower and change. Then meet us out in the living room. Time to start your training," he announced.

"My what?" I blinked in confusion as Simon turned to leave and Gene hopped into some pants, moving to follow.

Simon turned back to face me. "You're training to fight, of course. You did ask, and now, while you're all juiced up, is the perfect time."

I thrust out my lower lip in a pout. I was disappointed. What happened to morning nookie? Which I'd planned to follow with afternoon sex and evening decadence.

As if sensing my change in mood, Simon came back toward the bed. He leaned over me, his massive body annoyingly covered in clothes. His lips brushed against mine, and I twined my arms around his neck, trying to pull him down on top of me. It was like trying to move a boulder.

I gave up with a sigh. He gave me one last lingering kiss and moved away, but not before saying with a wink, "If you're a good girl at training, the reward will be well worth it."

And with that promise, I perked up. *I'll be the fastest freaking learner ever.*

I ate the breakfast Simon made me while talking to my roommates on my phone and giggling over my very successful date. Claire reminded me I was scheduled for work later, and much as I wanted to call in sick, the bills still needed paying. Once I'd cleared the tray of food, I hopped into the shower, soaping my body and wiping the scent of their lovemaking from my skin. I reassured myself with the thought they'd soon be dirtying me up again.

Emerging from the shower wearing nothing, I was tickled to find a yoga outfit waiting for me on the bed. I'd kind of hoped one of the boys would be in the room. With no one to seduce, I dressed in the comfortable clothes and running shoes before heading out into the main living area.

Gene was waiting for me, wearing matching exercise clothing. I looked around. "Where's Simon?"

"He was called away on some business. Never fear, he'll return soon. Now, are you ready to learn how to be the baddest hybrid misfit ever?"

I grinned. "Ready when you are, bottle boy."

Gene mock-scowled at me. "Those are fighting words, missy. Now get your delectable ass over here so I can take us to the training field."

"Can't we just visit your bottle?" I asked as I approached him with a come-hither smile.

He groaned. "Dammit, woman, stop tempting me. I promised Simon I'd teach you some basics, so stop throwing your womanly wiles at me, or I'll I put you over my knee."

"Promises, promises," I purred, sliding up to him and wrapping my arms around his neck. "Now I'll have to really make sure I'm *bad*," I said, kissing him.

The embrace was short-lived because the distinctive change in atmosphere made me open my eyes.

I pulled away from Gene in shock because we stood in a wasteland, a grey one that stretched endlessly in all directions. "Where on Earth are we?"

"Not Earth. Welcome to Limbo, the place between Heaven and Hell. Ancient history claims this once used to be a lush place, a neutral realm where all beings could get together where the only rule was respect for one another."

"What happened?" I whispered. This place, with its vast emptiness, tugged at something in me. I didn't understand it.

"War happened. Neutrality ended up getting trampled by the Army of Light and Legion of Darkness. Their clash destroyed this place, and history claims that when the greyness of nothing overtook this place, the walls that bound Heaven and Hell were erected."

"Can it not be fixed?" I asked. I could sense the anticipation of this place. It tickled along my senses.

"You cannot fix something dead," Gene said flatly.

I wanted to protest this place was far from dead.

*Can't he feel it?* Except I could see by his expression he didn't. Not sure what to make of that, I kept my mouth shut.

"Now where should we start?" Gene mused, rubbing his hands together.

The imp in me couldn't resist. I hooked my foot around his ankle and toppled him to the dusty ground. I pounced on him, straddling his groin—which was very happy to see me.

Gene flashed me a white grin before rolling me smoothly under him. "Surprising the enemy is good. But you need to follow up before they regain the upper hand." He thrust his hips at me, jolting my sex before jumping up and striding away.

I pouted.

He turned around and winked. "Show me what you've got. Simon says you can fight. Let's see it."

I got up slowly, miffed he'd rebuffed my advances. *Fine, he wants me to hand him his ass, then I shall strive to please.*

I sauntered at him while mentally calculating how to attack him. His age probably gave him experience, so I'd have to be sneaky. And I knew he was stronger than me. He'd proven that the night before to my orgasmic delight.

I'd almost reached him when he moved in an almost blur. My arms came up to block the blows he rained on me instinctively. I felt like Luke Skywalker using the force. I moved in my own blur, and I grinned.

The jerk upped the ante so that, every few moves, he landed a blow. Annoyed, I found my opening, and kicked him—in the nuts.

He groaned and folded. "Not fair," he gasped.

"Neither is making a half succubus work for sex," I retorted, placing my hands on my hips.

He staggered back to his feet, and we continued to spar. I was actually quite good at this. Surprise! While held prisoner, my brothers, few sisters, and I had often engaged in mock battles, sometimes to burn off energy, other times at the prodding of the scientists who wanted to see what we were capable of. I learned quickly how to fight—dirty. As a female, I just wasn't as big or strong as some of the others, so I learned how to stay on top by using every trick there was. From aiming for their manparts to using my girly wiles to distract them, I did what I had to in order to come out on top.

Like now, instead of stepping away from a shot Gene aimed at me, I took it in the shoulder and moved forward. I slipped an agile hand down the front of his pants and grabbed him, pleased to find him semi-erect and eager for my touch. He moaned and went still. I slid my hand up and down the length of his shaft and rubbed my cheek against his before whispering, "You're now dead." I clamped my mouth around his jugular, the tips of my pointy teeth pricking his skin.

"But what a way to die," he sighed.

I wanted to scream with frustration when he moved away from me, the evidence of his arousal tenting the front of his track pants.

"Now that we've ascertained you can handle hand-to-hand combat, time to see what else you can do."

"You mean like this?" With a little focus, my wings sprang from my back in a grey feathery cloud. I bounded up and, with a few full flaps, was airborne. I evened myself out in a few strokes and coasted on the strange aerial currents flowing through Limbo's grey skies. I pumped my wings and grinned, for flying truly was a treat. A flash of color made me turn my head, and in my shock at what I saw, I began to plummet. I quickly flapped my wings, regaining my height, and shook my head with a smile. "You are such a ham," I said to Gene.

He just grinned at me from where he sat cross-legged on a tasseled, brightly-colored rug.

"Let's see what you can do with those wings of yours," he said, leaning forward on his flying carpet. He poured on the speed and pulled away from me. I laughed and pumped to catch up. I followed him as he weaved, spun, and dove toward the ground.

Liberating didn't come close to describing it. In the human world, I had to be careful about when and where I used my aerial ability. During my captivity, the scientists had only allowed me to fly under the watchful eyes of snipers. Since my escape, any flying I did ended up restricted to moonless nights—alone.

With Gene, I could be myself, and we had fun, whooping and hollering as we chased each other through the grey sky. When a dark shadow covered me, I looked up and gaped. A massive dragon flew overhead, and as I watched, it opened its mouth and spewed out a cloud of white mist.

"Holy crap." Distracted, I lost altitude, and before I could flap to regain it, I found myself grasped in an icy claw. "Simon, that better be you," I warned. Actually, a part of me recognized him, not with my eyes or nose but more with my senses. My massive dragon lover landed and set me down on the ground.

I took several steps back and eyed him up and down. "Look at you. You're awesome."

The immense reptilian body was covered in shimmering white scales that glinted blue when he moved. His body was muscled, and his limbs ended in wickedly sharp claws. He had a long tail with barbs on the end, and a ridge of spines went up his back. The green eyes, while much larger, remained the same, and they regarded me with humor as I walked up to him. He lowered his head, and I rubbed his snout, even as I shivered at the sight of teeth that were the length of my arm.

"Hey, handsome, so when you change back into your man shape, will you be naked?" I asked with my one-track mind.

My dragon snorted, and beneath my petting hand, the body shrank and the scales melted into the skin of his face, which I'd grown intimately acquainted with the night before.

To my chagrin, he wore clothes. I must have made a moue of disappointment because he chuckled and dropped a light kiss on my lips. "Hello, darling. Nice wings."

"Thanks," I replied, ruffling them.

With a flourish I'd come to expect, Gene landed with his carpet, and Simon snorted. "Showoff."

Gene grinned. "Glad you could make it."

"How did you make it?" I asked. "I thought Gene was the one with transportation powers."

Simon rolled a shoulder. "I'm able to move between the planes, but I'm not as accurate as Gene, and it's much harder for me to bring along passengers."

"About time you arrived. I was just about to start testing her abilities to block metaphysical attacks."

"Whoa," I said, bringing my hands up. "Much as I'd love to see the different ways in which people, or things, can kill me, I've got to get ready for work."

Simon's brow crinkled. "But I thought we agreed you'd feed off us."

"Um, hello, I don't work just to feed, you know. I have bills to pay." Gene opened his mouth, and I stopped him with a glare. "No, I will not take money from you. That would be treating me like some kind of prostitute. I said I wouldn't feed off others, although that applies only to the touching kind. I will continue to feed off the emotions of my audience."

Simon looked like he would argue, but at a curt nod from Gene, he clamped his lips tight. "Very well. We will be around in case trouble crops up, so fear not, even if you don't see us. But know this," he said, coming close to me and staring down at me with his eyes glowing. "You will be spending the night with us."

I trembled with instant arousal and wished I had more time to get a sample of what I could see in his eyes. But Gene and I had spent quite a bit of time sparring, and according to my inner clock, it was time to get ready for work.

"I'll take her home," Gene offered.

Simon bent me over and gave me a thorough kiss that made me want to say screw work, but I fought his allure, to the disappointment of my body. Gene slipped his arm around my waist and, in surely the best method of transportation ever invented, popped us back into the human world just outside my apartment door.

"I gotta ask," I said, turning in his arms to face him. "How do you know when you teleport us that there's no one around to see?"

"I don't." He shrugged. "The magic seems to take care of that for me. Cool, huh?"

"Very." I leaned in for my goodbye kiss, which also included some ass groping, before I finally went in to face reality—and a thousand questions from my roomies.

But the biggest question of all, more like an epiphany, was my feelings for the guys.

*Fuck me, but I think I'm falling in love.*

## CHAPTER 9

THE CLUB WAS quiet that night, and true to their word, I didn't sense or see my boyfriends at all. And yeah, I giggled each time I thought or said the word boyfriends.

With all that happened, the last thing I wanted to do was dance, so I did my sets on autopilot, the trickle of emotion from the crowd nothing compared to what my lovers could give me.

Only a few days since I'd met them and already they'd ruined me. I'd never be able to return to feeding on humans. I wanted something more satisfying. I wanted Simon and Gene.

At the end of my second stage show, I found Claire wiping glasses behind the bar.

"Hey, I'm heading out," I announced.

She crinkled her nose. "I thought the boys would be picking you up."

So did I, and disappointed wasn't the word. Not that I let it show. I shrugged. "Guess their plans changed."

"Are you going to our place?"

"Probably." I certainly wasn't going to Simon's. A part of me feared I'd trusted too soon. Maybe all their words were just pretty lies. *No. I don't believe it.* Something must have delayed them.

"Be careful."

"Always," I replied with a carefree grin I didn't quite feel. Admitting to Claire I was worried about walking home wasn't going to happen. Then she'd insist on going with me, and quite honestly, if something did ambush me, I'd prefer my best friend not get turned into rabbit kebob.

Head held at an angle that screamed confidence—even if my insides quivered—I headed out, my high heels clacking on the pavement as I went up the street. A part of me kept expecting Gene or Simon to pop out and say "Boo," or at least slap my ass in hello, but the night was eerily silent.

So much for spending the night together. I wondered what had held them up. It better be important. I refused to give in to worry yet. Or doubts. Perhaps it was foolish of me, but, despite my past experiences, I truly wanted to trust Gene and Simon. I wanted to believe they wouldn't let me down without good reason.

My heels clacked noisily on the sidewalk, and given the deserted streets, I decided maybe a flight home would be in order. I'd no sooner thought it than I heard a whisper of sound. I whirled—too late. The coarse fabric of a sack was pulled over my head, and though I thrashed and kicked, steel bands wrapped around me, and when I felt the prick in my side, all I could think was, *Shit, not again.*

## CHAPTER 10

GRRR. Simon bit back a growl as he watched Beth taken down and manhandled by the vamps. It went against everything in him to let those dark beings just take her.

"Calm your beast. You know this is the best way to locate their lair," Gene said, placing a restraining hand on his arm.

"Doesn't mean I have to like it," muttered Simon, finding it hard to do nothing while he saw his woman attacked, drugged, and kidnapped.

"Save your fury for when we rescue her in a moment."

"And who's going to save us from Beth's fury?" Simon asked, arching a brow at his friend.

"I hope your tongue and cock are in working order when the battle is done because we'll have to make it up to her, probably more than once."

Simon, even given the seriousness of their mission, couldn't help remembering Beth. Not naked and panting, although she was beautiful in that moment. Nor with her lips wrapped around his cock, much as it pleased him. No, he remembered Beth's trust in him, a trust he'd protect her, and here he'd let some dirty vampires kidnap her. *I will make them pay for every hair they've bent,* he swore.

Quietly, he and Gene followed the vamps, who stuffed their unconscious prize into a dark, paneled van. Simon had wanted to shift into dragon shape to follow, but Gene talked him out of it, saying his beast was too large to squeeze between the narrow confines of the city streets. Instead, they rode Gene's carpet, not the colorful one he'd used in Limbo, but one dark as the night itself. It also matched Simon's mood. He consoled himself with the fact that once they killed all the dark ones, it would mean one less danger to Beth.

And only a freaking huge menace would be left to her in the form of the Legion of Darkness and Army of Light. He'd received some disturbing news while Gene had been busy training Beth.

It would seem both armies were aware of Beth's existence already. But another tidbit from his source gave him reason to hope, for he learned the two armies were divided on what to do. It seemed a large faction on both sides wanted to let the prophecy fulfill itself in the hopes of tearing down the walls that surrounded their realms. While many demons and angels could move freely in and out, nothing else could, not without the use of some powerful magic. Not to mention, ever since the walls had been erected, effectively sectioning the forces for good and evil, neutral no longer existed. You either belonged to one camp or the other, and many were tired of the whole freaking thing.

This fracture in the two realms was great news for Gene and Simon, as it meant less beings for them to destroy when the battle for Beth's survival occurred. And that was one thing everyone seemed to agree on. There would be a fight.

Gene nudged him as the van halted outside a large house tucked outside of town. The light flooding the front lawn from the windows was enough for them to see that there were quite a few cars parked on the curving driveway. The stench of vampire was unmistakable, especially to one with a refined olfactory sense like his.

"Time to play?" Simon questioned.

Gene grinned, his smile bright in the gloom. "Let's show them what happens when they mess with the woman of beings more powerful than them."

Simon jumped down from the floating carpet, hitting the ground with barely a thump. He flexed his hands, and his claws sprouted sharp and deadly.

*Time to kick some vampire ass so I can get some sweet ass of my own.* He sniffed the air and found his first victim, a fledgling left to guard outside.

With a twist and a crack that severed the spine, the vampire dropped to the ground, permanently dead. Not that Simon stayed to check. Urgency and a need to protect Beth took over, and the vampires he met on his path to find his woman discovered why they should never fuck with dragons—*because no one touches what is mine.*

When the outside was cleared of the foul ones, Simon met up with Gene who, with a flick of his hand, sent the front door to the home swinging open soundlessly.

In they stalked, Gene flicking fireballs at the vampires that came pouring out of the depths of the home to meet them. Simon took a more hands-on approach—slicing, dicing, and breaking the snapping creatures that dared get close enough to him. And when they began giving him a wide berth, he went after them with a snarl.

They worried not about the noise they made because Gene, in order to retain the element of surprise, dropped a silencing spell on the area.

At last, only one stupid vampire stood between him and the closed doors that hid Beth.

"Shall we announce ourselves? Gene asked with a deadly twinkle in his eyes.

Simon just grinned, and while the remaining vampire blanched—not an easy feat given his already pale status—he approached, rotating his extended claws in a hypnotizing swirl.

When he got close enough, he grabbed the soon-to-be permanently dead vampire and rammed a sharp claw through its torso. He allowed the creature to emit a scream that he cut off with a slice to its jugular.

Then he stood in front of the doors, chest heaving. A cry from inside made his rage double, and before he could barrel through the doors, Gene blasted them open.

And when he saw his Beth, tied to a chair with her face swelling, he lost all reason.

The primal roar he let loose needed no words because all understood its meaning. DIE!

## CHAPTER 11

CRACK. Ow.

I regained consciousness to a slap in the face. I forced my heavy eyelids open to see a familiar face—how unfortunate. "Jeremy, I should have known you'd be behind a cowardly attack on a woman."

My former compound brother, who during his incarceration with me had acted as a sort of leader to the rest of the inmates, grinned at me with pointed teeth. "Beth, how nice to see you again."

"I wish I could say the same. How'd you find me?" Of all my ex-brothers, Jeremy frightened me the most. As the strongest of the lab-created vamps, he was the one who'd received a sample of my blood, given to him by scientists who wanted to see what effect my blood would have on him. Jeremy had greatly enjoyed my blood because it not only gave him the ability to walk in sunlight, but it was apparently also much better tasting than that of a human's—lucky me. From that moment on, I ended up having to watch myself because, once word got around about my blood's unique properties, all the vampires incarcerated with me wanted a taste, whether I was willing or not.

"I've been looking for you a long time. I can't believe you didn't come with us when we escaped. I thought we were family."

"Family doesn't want to fuck and suck on each other," I spat. It still irked me that they'd turned on me. Silly me, I thought being victims of the same sick bastards would have made the bond of friendship stronger than that of avarice. I used to be so gullibly stupid back then.

"Minor details. As to how I found you, I noticed over the years that, every time one of us went missing, it coincided with them going out for some *fun*, the naked dancing on a pole kind. When I realized that, I began sending groups of the boys to clubs, although I have to admit, when you moved cities about two years ago, you almost lost me. Lucky me, though, I found you again."

"Yeah, lucky." As I encouraged Jeremy to talk, I worked at the rope that bound me to the chair I sat on. But my claws, while sharp, were awkwardly placed for slicing. I also wondered what the hell had happened to my supposed protectors. They'd put me out there as bait and then disappeared. Nice. They'd have some apologizing to do with their tongues and cocks when I got out of here. Of course, the odds of my escaping didn't look good, but I always was an optimist.

"Aren't you going to ask what I have planned?" Jeremy said with a smile that said without words that nobody sane was home.

"Hmm, let me guess, you've decided to bathe. Or is

that just wishful thinking on my part?" I wrinkled my nose and was rewarded with an expression of rage and a backhand that snapped my head sideways. I saw pretty stars for a moment before I straightened to taunt him again. "Ooh, what a big man, hitting a woman all tied up. Is that the only way you get sex, too?"

I expected the next slap, and I laughed once the buzzing in my ears died down. "Woo. I was wrong. Even tied up, a woman is too feisty for you."

Jeremy's eyes burned red with rage, and I smiled vapidly back at him. I knew from experience my succubus wiles didn't work on him, something about his mind or powers being too strong. But it didn't stop me from sending out vibes in the hopes some of his weaker coven members would succumb and give me an edge.

"Nice try." Jeremy smirked. "I've learned a lot in the last couple of years, including how to control those weaker than me, which happens to be all of the vamps that came with me and those I've come across since."

"It didn't help Jonathon," I replied sassily.

Jeremy growled. "Let me rephrase then. So long as they're within a certain proximity, I can protect their minds from soul-sucking bitches like you."

"Oh, that's rich coming from a blood sucker." I rolled my eyes. A crash sounded from outside the room, along with a scream that cut off abruptly. A chill breeze flowed into the room with a familiar scent, and I smiled. "Uh-oh, are you in big trouble now."

Jeremy slapped me again, and I cried out on purpose, for truly, the slap hadn't actually hurt much. But I achieved the desired result.

The doors to the room slammed open, and in stalked my furious dragon, his body bulging at the seams and his green eyes blazing with fury. Gene followed behind him with his trademark grin, juggling fireballs. Even given my current predicament, I found it hot, and my body responded.

Simon spied me, and I could tell by the way his body tensed up that he'd noticed the swelling on my face.

"Hey, baby," I called out. "He did it." I inclined my head toward Jeremy, who blanched when, with a roar that shook the house, Simon charged at him.

Gene followed more slowly, lobbing fireballs with unerring accuracy at the other vampires scattered about the room. When he finally reached me and released my bonds, I couldn't resist saying, "Took you long enough. I thought I was going to have to clean the nest up by myself."

"I tried to hold Simon back because I knew you could handle it, but dragons can't stand it when people steal from them." Gene rolled his eyes as he said it while, at the same time, lobbing a fireball over my shoulder.

Something screamed and gurgled, a sound covered by Simon roaring again. "Should we help him?" I asked as I watched Simon decapitate a vampire to get at Jeremy, who'd hidden behind rows of his people.

"Nah. He needs to blow off some steam. He wasn't crazy about the plan." Gene tossed that tidbit at me casually.

"Gee, and did it never occur to you to let me know about the plan?" I placed my hands on my hips and glared at him.

Gene grinned and shrugged. "What, and miss the fun we'll have making it up to you?"

I punched him in the arm and laughed. "You are incorrigible."

I thought about joining the fight, but was much more intrigued watching my big, badass dragon work on his anger issues. The man moved with a breath-taking grace, and while his fury was bloody, I loved that he was furious on my behalf. It didn't take long for Simon to finish dealing with his vengeance, and at the end of it all, there was an impressive scattering of dead vampires.

With the source of his anger eliminated, Simon stalked toward me, still bristling, almost seven feet of sweaty male—oh my. I didn't flinch, even when he grabbed me in a bear hug that squeezed all the breath from me.

"I'm okay," I squeaked.

"He hit you," growled Simon.

"It's healing already," I replied, loving his concern.

"I'm going to kill him again," he said, putting me down before turning to glare at Jeremy's corpse.

"Couldn't we just set the place on fire and then go back to your place to do the same with your sheets?"

I assumed the fact that he threw me over his shoulder meant yes. I'll admit the position had its merits, such as an interesting view of his ass, which I pinched, with difficulty. The man was built like a rock.

He responded with a smack on my bottom that made me squirm.

"Ow," I said, more out of habit than pain.

"That will teach you to mouth off to bad guys and get hurt before I have a chance to rescue you."

Really? I slapped his ass back. "And that," I replied, "was for coming up with a plan that involved me without telling."

"Children," said Gene, jogging up beside us. "Can we continue this fascinating slap and tickle play at home? This place is about to go up in smoke."

Sure enough, while Simon and I squabbled, Gene had proved a busy bee, lobbing fireballs about the place and setting it on fire. Given the age of the structure—old and ugly—it would burn well, leaving no signs, recognizable human ones anyway, of the vamps that had used it as a lair.

In what was becoming a familiar threesome hug, Gene popped us back to the loft.

Once there, though, Simon didn't put me down. On the contrary, he stomped into the bathroom and turned on the shower.

"What are you doing?" I asked, starting to get tired of my upside-down position.

"Washing the stench of that creature off you."

Mmm, that sounded promising. Simon finally set me back on my feet, and his strong hands made short work of my clothes to the detriment of the seams.

Gene sauntered in as Simon turned me to and fro, inspecting me for damage.

"I'm fine."

Simon just growled and continued to run his hands down my body, which I enjoyed, so I didn't protest much.

I did yelp, however, when Gene gave my bare ass a

slap. "Hey." I turned my head to glare at him. His eyes glowed with desire, and the hint of a smile curving his lips made my heart rate speed up.

"Get in the shower before I give you another one."

I blew him a kiss and didn't move. I even waggled my bottom at him. The sharp smack tingled, and my budding arousal went into all-out arousal mode.

"Naughty girl," Simon murmured, his voice thick. I looked up at him and melted at the hungry look in his face.

I found myself manhandled into the oversized shower, the hot spray striking skin sensitized with anticipation. In short order, my lovers joined me.

Gene stood before me, his curved cock jutting from his groin. "Bend over and taste it," he ordered.

I did as ordered—eagerly. I folded my body over, sticking my bottom out for Simon's visual enjoyment. I took Gene's swollen head into my mouth, moaning when his fingers grasped my hair, guiding me.

Behind me, Simon took up position, the head of his shaft brushing my backside. I wiggled it, longing to feel the thickness of his prick as it stretched my channel.

What I got instead was a slap. I cried out around the rod in my mouth and only barely managed to not bite down. Gene's hands tightened their grip on my hair, pushing me back and forth on his length. He matched his rhythm to the rain of smacks on my bottom, something I'd never actually indulged in before but was rapidly discovering I enjoyed. I moaned as my ass heated up, the tingle of the slaps Simon bestowed firing my libido and soaking my pussy.

The sudden thrust of his massive cock into my channel forced me forward onto Gene's prick, driving it down my throat, where my muscles flexed convulsively.

Gene's grip on my scalp tightened, and through gritted teeth, he panted, "Take what you need."

I didn't know which side of me he meant, but the decision was taken from me when my sharp incisors lowered, scraping the tender skin of his shaft.

Hot coppery liquid hit my tongue, and I sucked at it, taking what he offered and more. My more sensual side woke as my dark feeding aroused me even further. My erotic delight passed from me to Gene, a molten wave of bliss that, combined with the pounding pleasure of Simon's cock in my pussy, brought on my orgasm. I cried out around the shaft in my mouth, taking him deep and clamping down.

"Oh fuck," Gene groaned before shooting his fiery load down my throat.

I was too busy to enjoy his reaction, though, still caught in the waves of my diminishing climax. Simon continued to pump me, his rod a tight fit, but one that I loved. Distracted by Simon's actions, I couldn't stop Gene's sated cock from slipping out of my mouth. He didn't seem to mind, as he knelt under my bent body and caught a protruding nipple with his mouth, tugging it hard and sending a pleasurable jolt right down to my cleft. One orgasm down, I could already feel the next one building.

Behind me, Simon continued to slap my buttocks as he rammed me, the zinging pain making my pelvic muscles tighten deliciously around his shaft. I froze, though, when he stroked his thumb over my puckered ring.

I looked over my shoulder and gasped, "Out hole."

His blazing eyes met mine. "For now."

Gene released my nipple long enough to say, "Oh, sweet one, wait until you experience the ecstasy of having both of us seated in you at the same time. Our hard cocks fucking both your tight holes, our bodies sandwiching yours." Then having said his piece, he bit down on my nub, and I cried out.

When he put it like that, I had to admit the idea had its appeal, even given my preconceived—if strange—notions about acceptable sex. Simon, as if sensing the direction of my thoughts, popped his thumb right into my rosette, a shocking maneuver that, even in its alien feel, brought on my climax.

Gene's lips caught my ecstatic scream as my body convulsed and quivered in the throes of pleasure, a bliss that went on and on, and Simon somehow, through his rod, seated deep inside, fed me his arousal. When with a mighty bellow, he finally came, I was overwhelmed with the power that rushed into me and collapsed against Gene, who held me cradled in his arms as the water in the shower, now gone tepid, continued to pour over us. And even though we ended up washing each other with giggles under a chilly spray, one thought kept circling.

*Hot damn, I'll have to try and be bad more often if this is how they intend to punish me.*

## CHAPTER 12

THE NEXT MORNING, I smiled wider than the Cheshire Cat. My expanding sexual horizons and my adept lovers had me feeling better—and more powerful—than I ever remembered.

Unlike my previous wakeup, I got the morning nookie I craved, a quick, sweaty tag-team affair where Simon and Gene kept swapping position between my legs. But the climax was worth it, even if it left me in desperate need of a shower before I went home trailing the scent of sex after me.

I dressed in another new outfit courtesy of the guys, which I didn't argue about, given they kept destroying my clothes in their eagerness to claim me. Ain't love grand?

The brush I was using fell from suddenly numb fingers as I froze.

Love? Could it be?

I thought over how Gene and Simon made me feel, and not just in the bedroom. I mulled over the conversations we had, many of which weren't comprised of sexual innuendo. I pondered the fact that I missed them like crazy when we were apart. I couldn't deny the facts stacking up.

*Oh shit, I'm in love.*

On the heels of that amazing revelation, fear followed. *But what if they don't feel the same way?*

Compared to them, I was an inexperienced babe in the woods. How could I hope to keep their attention outside the bedroom? I knew nothing of the things they'd gone through. I held maybe a fraction of their knowledge.

Even as all the reasons for them to not love me piled up, one thing kept intruding—my gut instinct. And that internal dousing rod of mine, also known as female intuition, said they cared for me, and possibly loved me as much as I loved them.

How and when should I tell them, though? Somehow, just walking out into the living room and announcing it aloud seemed wrong. The moment I declared myself should have meaning or, at the very least, attempt to be special. I should also plan a quick escape route should I be totally mistaken and they not return my affection.

I finished with my toilette and walked out into the main living area. My men turned like one person, even though they stood on opposite sides of the room, and their smiles of welcome warmed me and melted my doubts.

*They care, and when the moment's right, I'm going to tell them what I feel.*

We joked and chatted over breakfast, the only somber moment coming when Simon and Gene mentioned meeting with the forces aligned against those in Heaven and Hell who would see me dead.

"So does this mean we're going to war?" I asked.

"Hopefully not. If we can show the Legion of Darkness and the Army of Light that we outnumber them, then maybe we can avert an all-out battle."

I had my doubts, but I wouldn't rain on Simon's optimism. I knew he did all this for one reason only—to protect me.

All too soon, Simon was kissing me goodbye with promises to meet up with me later. I didn't bother calling my roomies to warn them I was coming. I just had Gene drop me off.

I hugged him to me tightly, an odd sense of uneasiness making me say, "You'll be careful?"

"Don't fear for me. I am much harder to kill than you'd think." Not exactly reassuring words, but apparently it was the best I'd get. He kissed me soundly. "See you in a few hours. And remember, if you need me, just make a wish."

His words warmed me, even as he popped out of sight. How did I ever get so lucky?

I swallowed that internal thought when I walked into chaos. The apartment looked like a herd of animals had rampaged through it. A rotten egg miasma in the air made me pull my shirt up over my nose to filter the smell, but it did nothing to block the visual chaos.

The cushions on the couch were scattered and torn. Broken glass glittered all over the floor and went well with the shredded books. My heart sped up, not in fear for myself but in trepidation for my friends, who should have both been home.

Maybe they weren't here when it happened. I walked farther into the scene of destruction, trying to momentarily deny the inevitable conclusion. The message scrawled on the wall of the dining room took my last hope away.

The blood they'd use to write still glistened wetly and even ran in rivulets in some spots.

*We have your friends. If you want them to live, then you will exchange yourself for them. Tell no one or they will die.*

I clenched my fists to keep from screaming, my elongating nails biting deep into my palms. In all the scenarios that I'd run through my head, I'd never actually imagined anyone coming after my friends. They were innocent, and I was even more naïve.

My first impulse was to call the guys for help, but the blatant threat stayed my hand. I wouldn't be responsible for their deaths, not when their only fault had been to befriend a hybrid misfit.

Tears threatened to spill as I realized what I needed to do—and my choice wouldn't please my lovers. However, if I wanted to die, my conscience free and clear knowing I'd done the right thing, then I needed to act as I saw fit.

Decision made, I wondered how I was supposed to find the bastards who'd kidnapped and, judging by the blood, harmed my friends.

I approached the macabrely painted wall and saw, embedded in the plaster, a slim dagger pinning a piece of paper. I yanked the blade out and grabbed at the note as it fluttered down.

*Blood shall get you to where you need to go.*

Great. I held the sharp edge over the palm of my hand, but hesitated.

*Can I really do this? Go willingly to my death?*

It tore at me. All my life I'd fought against that invisible specter, and now that I'd finally beaten the Grim Reaper, Murphy's Law had caught up to me and was laughing in my face. I thought of my friends. Lana, who deserved a chance to sing and eventually embrace her siren side. And dear Claire, whose cute bunny side deserved someone to love and cuddle her. I couldn't sentence them to death.

The dagger cut cleanly into the palm of my hand, and red blood welled up, coating the blade, which warmed in my grip.

Unlike Gene's seamless form of transportation, this method wrenched my body in what seemed like every direction at once, and with a sickening lurch, I left to meet my fate—and greet death after running for so long.

# CHAPTER 13

"THE TIME IS NOW," Gene boomed, his voice amplified by magic. Not that he truly needed to, considering those he addressed had power enough on their own to hear him if they wished.

The king of the gnomes stood, his red pointed hat giving him a height he would have otherwise lacked. "Attack without provocation? It is one thing to retaliate, but to go preemptively on the offensive seems foolish."

Simon growled. "So you would sit here while they plan the death of the one person who may fulfill the prophecy?"

The little man scoffed. "And if she's not the one? Are we prepared to rile the forces of Heaven and Hell just because you like the taste of her honey pot?"

A roar burst free from Simon, and he would have leapt on the gnome had Gene not held him back.

Gene, however, felt the same frustration as Simon. The time had come for them to stop cowering and take a stand. Yes, part of their reason was selfish. He and Simon both loved Beth, but it was more than that. After several millennia of division, it was time to look for a better way, and regardless of what the gnome king said, sitting back and waiting was not an option.

Apparently, he wasn't the only one who thought so.

Queen Mab stood in all her splendid, golden glory, and before her powerful gaze, all quieted and waited for her to speak. "The Ifrit and Ice Dragon are correct. We can no longer allow this state to continue. The walling of Heaven and Hell, the separation of good and evil, has to stop. Do we know for sure this girl is the one? No, but if she is, and we do nothing, in effect allowing her to be killed, then we may lose our chance to restore the balance. So I ask you again, are you with us or not?"

Gene held his breath as he waited for the response. By throwing her support behind them, Mab had effectively silenced those who would have sat on the sidelines. Her words challenged them and also made it clear that those who abstained would not be kindly regarded.

His sigh of relief was washed away by the voices that rang out, promising their support. Simon slapped Gene on the back, and Gene almost fell over with his friend's enthusiasm.

At his core, Gene knew he should be happier, but he couldn't dispel a sense of unease. He longed to escape this tedious back and forth game the rulers played and check on Beth. *She's fine, and I'm turning into Simon, worrying about her safety all the time. Besides, if she needed me, she'd make a wish.*

But no matter his reassurance to himself, he couldn't stop the niggling doubt, and judging by Simon's faraway expression, he wasn't alone.

But politics forced him away from his unease.

## CHAPTER 14

I LANDED in Limbo on my knees, dry heaving and spitting. Not exactly an elegant way to arrive.

"And this is the abomination who is supposed to change Heaven and Hell?" said a guttural voice. The question was followed by a kick in my ribs. The force of the blow threw me back, and I lay on the dusty ground, sucking in air.

A musical voice that would have sounded beautiful if not for the condescension in its tone replied, "Yes, it's hard to believe this human-born creature has the power to destroy the status quo."

Their insults really annoyed me. Wasn't it enough I'd bravely decided to trade myself for my friends? Did they have to degrade me, too?

I sprang to my feet as anger fired up my adrenaline. I found myself facing the epitomes of good and evil.

On the left, there was a huge black demon, replete with horns, coal-red eyes, and a general nasty demeanor.

On the right was perfection itself in the form of a male angel with curly blond ringlets, eyes of a summer blue sky, dressed in a white gown, the purity of which matched that of the angel's outspread wings. What a shame the pretty exterior didn't extend to its interior.

It baffled me that a creature thought to be good could be involved in something so evil, but as my father had once told me, good and evil were all in the perception of the perpetrator. I hadn't understood what he'd tried to explain at the time, but the wisdom he'd imparted made sense later when I met the doctors who experimented on me. They, too, thought they worked for the good of man. I disagreed.

But questions of right and wrong would have to wait. I had a more important mission. "Where are my friends?" I asked boldly.

The two beings stepped aside, and I saw my friends, tied to stakes with gags stuffed in their mouths. Claire, with a cut on her temple, stared at me with eyes round with fright, her cheeks marked with tears. Lana, her face battered, looked fierce, and I knew, if she could free herself, she'd say to hell with giving up. She'd fight to the death.

My heart squeezed tight. "I came as you asked. Now let them go."

Then came the answer I'd expected. "Why would we do that?" replied the demon. "Once you're dead, I look forward to taking the feisty one back to Hell with me. While Gabriel here has shown an interest in the little bunny."

"That wasn't the deal." My fury bubbled inside of me. Had it just been me against the demon and angel, I was pretty sure I'd prevail, but behind my friends, I could see the demonic horde on one side and the angelic detachment on the other.

*Hot damn, just what is it they're afraid I can do? That's some serious backup considering they're just going up against one hybrid misfit.*

I wanted to know why they feared me. And then I wanted to make it come true. I'd had plenty of time to ponder the words of the prophecy, and I had a theory, one that hadn't fully formed until I found myself in Limbo again.

All around me, the greyness called to me. It sent tingles throughout me, and I could almost hear it whisper. *Blood.*

A plan unfolded in my mind. The odds of it succeeding were pretty slim and relied on several unknowns, but the consequences of doing nothing loomed over me even worse.

The demon laughed. "And who are you going to tell? You came here alone, you stupid Nephilim."

"I am not a Nephilim," I stated. I pushed my wings out with a shower of grey feathers and straightened my spine. The angel Gabriel's eyes widened. I tilted my chin stubbornly. "I am a Hybrid Misfit, and I am done taking shit from either one of you. If you won't free my friends, then I guess I'll do it myself."

I launched myself in the air before they could grab me and, with a rapid flap of my wings, hurtled toward my friends. I yanked the dagger I'd hidden on my person when I'd arrived under the guise of puking and sliced at the bonds that held my friends.

I'd no sooner pulled Claire's gag free when she shouted, "Behind you!"

With her warning, I ducked without looking and swept my feet in a semicircle. I snagged the black demon, who staggered, revealing the angel with a gleaming sword behind him. I rolled on the dusty ground, vaguely noticing a rumble. I hopped up to my feet and sprinted away from my friends in the hopes of luring my foes after me.

It worked, kind of. While Gabriel and his demon friend stalked me with furious eyes, I could see their respective armies advancing on my friends.

I wanted to scream in frustration. But I hadn't given my friends enough credit, for while Claire was a bunny and low on the food chain, Lana wasn't.

Free of her gag and more pissed than I'd ever seen her.

I halted and gaped as a sudden breeze, smelling strongly of brine, ruffled her green-tinged hair. I could see her aura swell as she gathered power. Then she opened her mouth and sang.

Even though her melody wasn't directed at me, I staggered under the weight of her anger. It halted the advancing army in its tracks, but not the two advancing on me.

The moment had arrived. Did I fulfill the prophecy in the way I'd deciphered it, or did I call for help and postpone this moment to another time?

*I am not a coward. And I'm tired of running.*

I met the angel and demon, my grey wings and clothing a symbolic mix of the two strains of DNA bound to me. I was neither good nor evil. I was just me, something in the middle. I danced for my survival. Hopping and twisting to avoid the fatal blows they threw at me, I waited for my moment.

There to the left, I saw it. I raised my arm and blocked the black slashing claws of the demon. Burning pain shot up my arm as he opened a large gash in my flesh, the blood instantly welling. My arm fell limply to my side just as the angel with his silvery sword sliced at my other unprotected arm.

I grinned as I sank to the ground on my knees, my blood spraying from my matching wounds. I peered up at the beings, one so ugly it hurt and the other so bright it hurt even more. "Thank you," I said through the pain scalding its way through my system.

The demon frowned at me, but the angel's eyes opened wide, and he stared down at my blood, which dripped in fat plops onto the grey, dusty ground.

In the background, I faintly heard Lana singing as I stared down at the lifeless surface that soaked up my blood like a sponge. Drank my life essence and yet gave nothing in return.

I realized, a tad too late, that my theory was perhaps wrong. *I don't understand. I translated the fairy queen's words: Hail the blessed one for her blood shall destroy the boundaries.* I was certainly bleeding, but unfortunately, I didn't hear or see any sign that I'd fulfilled anything other than my own death.

Weakness permeated my limbs, and I slumped

forward onto the dusty ground as my life force leached from me to disappear into the parched wasteland. The shadows of the pair who'd struck the killing blows covered me.

Now, at the hour of my death, I made a wish. *Gene, I need you.*

## CHAPTER 15

THE REDUNDANT BICKERING by those attending the meeting made Simon want to coat the entire council chamber in frost. Could they not set their petty differences aside and grasp the bigger picture? They needed to act, not posture. Perhaps he'd let loose some of his frozen power and poke them—with the hard jab of an icicle—to move things along.

Gene stiffened beside him.

"What is it?" Did his friend suffer the same unease?

"We need to go now," the Djinn announced. "Beth's in trouble."

No more needed to be said. Simon clasped his friend's shoulder, and without a word of warning to the assembly, they popped dimensions right into a scene of nightmare.

And noise.

Simon winced as a siren's song vibrated loudly around them. It took only a moment to take in the scene, and it wasn't hard to figure out what had happened, given the players.

The stakes with hanging strands of rope stood sentry to Lana, who sang her siren's heart out. Claire, brandishing a dagger, stood by her friend, protecting her from two armies that, while frozen for the moment, were fighting against the siren's spell. All that, however, paled at the sight of Beth's form crumpled on the ground. Even worse, the figures of a demon and angel stood over her, their arms lifted to deliver fatal blows.

He let his fury go. "No!" With a roar of rage that thundered and shook the ground, his dragon burst forth. It startled the pair who thought to end his mate's life, and he gave a snaggle-tooth grin as they turned to face them with their puny weapons.

Frost puffed from his lips as he breathed, "Die!"

Simon wasn't the only one enraged. Gene finally lost his cool, his human form disappearing in puff of smoke to reveal his true Ifrit shape. A massive black cloud with glowing eyes appeared and Gene's voice boomed. "Death to the ones who hurt my beloved. War to those who supported them!"

The dragon bellowed in agreement, the ground before him frosting a path to the two whose life would be measured in seconds. Gene whirled from the leaders, leaving them to Simon's mercy—or lack thereof. While the Djinn threw devastating bombs at the armies, Simon lumbered after the heads of the angelic and demonic forces. Ice dragons did not often get involved in the wars of others, but when they did, no one survived. The angel and demon knew this. They scurried from him like the lowest of roaches.

*Fight me.*

Was it his words or the realization they could not escape? Whatever the reason, the cowards finally stopped scurrying to face him. Simon spared them no quarter. He inhaled and blew out, directing the stream of icy breath. He froze the demon and angel and turned them into living sculptures, unable to move, unable to scream, but able to see their destiny approaching. Simon grinned, a fearsome sight on his dragon visage, and then, with a sweep of his paw, he shattered them.

Turning about to aid Gene in destroying the armies who'd gathered, he discovered the tides had changes. Their newly found allies from the meeting had joined them. Ranks of fairies, gnomes, dwarves, and a host of other creatures advanced on the armies of Heaven and Hell, who, in turn, backed away, their resolve wavering without their leaders to bolster it.

A flutter of movement caught Simon's eye, and he turned only to have his eyes caught by Beth's still corpse. His rage evaporated in a wave of grief, and he shrank back into his male form. He'd barely changed before he was running to her side. He knelt beside her.

Across from her prone body, Gene fell to his knees as well.

"Oh, Beth," he whispered.

Simon couldn't stand to see her lying face-first in the dirt. Gently, he turned her body with Gene's aid so she lay on her back.

He couldn't stop his tears from falling, and they fell on the blood-soaked ground sprouting green grass.

What the fuck? He no sooner thought this than shit happened.

As Simon watched with disbelieving eyes, the green fuzz spread outwards from Beth's body, and the blood pooled around it. Simon stood to look and watched as the vivid emerald color rolled across the open plain, its shocking appearance stopping the combatants in their tracks as they watched with slack jaws.

But grass wasn't all that grew. From the ground turned green, vegetation sprouted. Flowers in a rainbow of colors popped free of the long-dead soil, along with twigs that grew into small saplings that then sprouted leaves of every color.

Simon pivoted, his eyes tearing as he realized that, in giving her life, Beth had woken Limbo. And when the ground quaked a few moments later, it wasn't hard to surmise that the walls penning Hell and Heaven, good and evil, had come down.

*She's freed everyone.* The tenure of good and evil was over. There was middle ground once again. He wished he could be happier at the thought that she hadn't died in vain, but he was a dragon and selfish. He would have forsaken just about anyone or anything to have her alive.

A gust of wind blew up out of nowhere, and he turned at the tickling breeze's insistence. He gasped at what he saw.

Beth floated above the ground in an upright position. Her arms were spread wide and her head tilted back. She wore a beatific smile, and when she opened her eyes, they blazed with a violet light. He sank to his knees, his eyes brimming with tears. Later he'd castigate himself for being less than manly. Right now, he couldn't contain his joy.

*My mate lives.*

## CHAPTER 16

I HONESTLY THOUGHT I was going to die. I lay there face-first in the ground and listened to Lana sing, cursing my stupidity.

When the boys arrived at my call, it broke my heart to hear the anguish in their voices as they beheld me. I wanted to lift my head and tell them I wasn't gone yet. But that took too much effort.

Instead, I closed my eyes, and in the grayness of my mind, the tingle that was Limbo became more pronounced. Having my blood bonded with the soil of this place had deepened my connection with it, and more than ever, I could sense the life that brimmed just below the surface.

*Well, what are you waiting for?* I asked.

As my heartbeat slowed, I realized what it wanted. Me.

*I've given you my blood. I'm about to give you my life. What else do you want?*

The answer, so simple, would have made me laugh had I not rested on the brink of death.

I agreed to the terms.

My choice made, the snowball I set in motion started rolling and changing the world as we all knew it.

The pain that bit so deep into me faded as my body knit itself back together, a gift for the deal I'd made. My heart sped up, and the hard ground beneath me disappeared as the power I set in motion lifted me on invisible wings. I opened my arms wide and took what Limbo, almost an entity in itself, gave me. My lips curved into a smile as it taught me what I needed to know.

Then I opened my eyes and beheld the new realm —my realm.

The first thing I noticed was the color—vivid color everywhere, but on the heels of that, I saw the stricken faces of my lovers. Poor Simon on his knees and Gene, looking gray under his tan.

"You are in so much trouble, my darling," Gene said in a shaky voice.

I smiled and laughed. "If it's anything like last time, I can't wait."

My body drifted down until my feet touched the new ground of the world I'd helped create. Not that I touched it for long because Simon swept me up in a dragon hug of massive proportions.

"Don't you ever scare me like that again," he whispered fiercely in my ear.

"Okay," I squeaked.

He might have never let me go—which was fine with

me—but Lana and Claire came running up and insisted on hugs of their own.

Claire had quickly rediscovered her bounce, even given their ordeal. "Oh, wow, that was totally cool the way you came in like some Lone Ranger with wings and flew to our rescue."

I cringed, knowing my lovers probably wouldn't see it in the same light, and judging by Simon's whispered, "That's going to earn you a punishment," I was going to reap the benefits later.

Lana also gave me a fierce hug. "Thanks for coming."

"I would never have forsaken you," I whispered back in a tight voice. "And damn, that was some wicked singing."

"Don't remind me," Lana moaned, pulling away.

I frowned. "Why? It was because of you that things ended up working out. Without you stopping the armies like that, we would all have been dead before the cavalry arrived."

"Yeah, well, it also made that dude over there think that I'm his fated mate or something."

I looked where she pointed and saw a blond giant, wearing a loin cloth, with an impressive bare chest, watching my friend avidly. I grinned. "Hot damn, Lana, I say go for it."

I laughed at her glare, but despite her attitude, I noticed her glancing often over at the goliath. Could it be my friend had found herself a boyfriend at last?

Happy as I was everything had turned out all right, I trembled with hunger, and not for the type that went in my belly. Not willing to wait, I tugged on Simon's hand,

and he leaned down so I could whisper in his ear. "I need you and Gene, now." Seeing the golden queen heading toward us along with others, I hastened to add the sugar that would sweeten the pot. "And if you can do it quick enough while still getting my friends home safe, I'll let you guys sandwich me."

As magic words went, it worked wonders. Quicker than I would have credited, I found myself, showered, naked, and in bed while reassured that my friends had plenty of help righting their destroyed apartment. Although I wasn't sure how Lana would feel, especially when I found out the giant blond had insisted on being in the group of volunteers. But I had bigger cocks to fry in the form of two testosterone-laden males with lustful intent in their expression eyeing me. How delightful.

I opened my arms wide and, with a cheeky smile, said, "So are you guys flipping for holes?" Naughty me, though I really hoped Gene with his slimmer cock got the virgin one.

They dove on me with hot, seeking mouths. Their dual latch on my budding nipples made me cry out. I grabbed at their heads, but they apparently decided they wanted to be in charge, for they each flung out a hand to grab mine and hold it down. And, yes, it was as hot as it sounded.

Pinned and helpless beneath their questing tongues, I gave into my building pleasure, panting and writhing in need. Simon left Gene to torture my nipples, his teeth nipping and pulling at them. My pussy tightened at his rough play while my honey seeped to soak the sheets—that was until Simon's tongue found my pink slit. He lapped at me, his tongue alternatively flicking my clit and delving into my sex.

I cried out at their torture of my sensitive body. They played my erogenous zones with masterful precision, stringing out my pleasure. At the peak, I found myself free of male mouths and flipped onto my stomach.

"Get on your hands and knees," Simon growled.

I complied with heaving breaths. I couldn't help tightening when I felt hands spreading my buttocks, and I bit my lip at the cold, oily liquid that dripped down the crack of my ass.

Gene's slender fingers swirled the fluid around my rosette, his light pokes not forcing their way, and I relaxed. Simon's blunt fingers found my silken slit and probed me. I clenched my channel around them as he pumped me. So relaxed was I that, when Gene popped a finger into my ass, with ease, I didn't buck away. He worked his finger back and forth, and while the pressure of it felt odd, with Simon's fingers still pumping my sex, I actually kind of enjoyed it.

Gene slipped a second finger in, and I stilled, for this increased the stretching sensation, but Simon used his thumb to stroke over my clit. The stimulation made me rock back against the fingers that probed me, and like a signal, Simon shifted his body until he lay under me.

I gazed down into his heavy-lidded eyes and kissed the sensual smile on his lips.

Against my mouth, he murmured, "Sit on my cock. Ride me, baby."

Like I needed any urging. With Gene's fingers still inserted in my ass, I lowered my body until my sex nudged the head of Simon's cock. Simon's hand came up to grab my waist, and impatient at my teasing, he drove me down onto his solid length. My hands, braced on his chest, dug in, and I threw my head back at the feeling of having him fully seated inside me. Under his urging hands, I rocked on his pelvis, the grinding sensation providing an erotically welcome friction to my swollen clit.

I mewled with loss when Gene withdrew his fingers. The head of his turgid shaft took their place, though, pushing at my rosette. Slowly, he guided it in, and I whimpered at the stretching. Doubts assailed me. *I don't think it will fit. Maybe we should...*

My fear fled when Simon found my clit and rubbed it, the pleasurable jolts making me sigh and relax. And then Gene was inside me.

I stilled at the strangeness of it. Simon's hands grabbed mine, pulling me down onto him, the position spreading my cheeks for Gene. He folded himself over top of me, his cock pushing into my ass even deeper. Sandwiched between their male bodies, I trembled.

Then they moved. One in, one out. They found a pace where they alternated their thrusts, and I ended up lost in a maelstrom of pleasure. They poured their arousal into me, feeding my succubus side while ramping up my own desire. When Simon bared his throat for me, I took his offered gift and bit his skin, tasting the life force he offered, and with so many of my needs being taken care of, in such a delightful manner, I shattered. My body bucked, or tried to. Caught between them, I couldn't escape the rapture that erupted throughout my body. My pussy convulsed so hard I expected Simon to cry out in pain, but instead, with a bellow of fierce elation, he came in shuddering jets, quickly followed by Gene in my not-so-virgin-anymore hole.

It was beyond fantastic. And I never wanted the feeling to end.

After a night of orgasms that I didn't have enough fingers and toes to count, I awoke feeling like a million bucks. And I owed it all to the two lugs sleeping on either side of me.

"Wake up," I shouted, laughing when Simon dove out of bed, stark naked, his eyes and hair wild.

Gene just stretched lazily and grinned. "Morning, gorgeous. Your wish is my command."

"Get over here," I ordered Simon, patting the bed beside me.

With a sheepish smile, he crawled back into bed, but before he could snag me with a thick arm, I scooted out from between them. I turned and sat on my haunches so I could see them both. Then I got shy, the words I wanted to say freezing in my throat.

"I—um," I stuttered, trying to spit it out. This was so stupid. I knew how I felt. Why couldn't I just say it? I took a deep breath. "I was going to make a great big speech, but screw it. I love you both and, if the offer is still open, would love to move in." I didn't tell them, though, that we'd eventually end up living in Limbo as part of my deal with it. Besides, it would surely take a few months to rebuild the city that Limbo said I'd need to inhabit, plenty of time to get them to see things my way.

Shocked silence met me, and I instantly regretted my

bold words. Only for a nanosecond, though, because then two naked male bodies hurtled themselves at me for a quick kiss. And then dove past me.

I looked at them dressing in bewilderment. "Um, don't you guys want to say something?"

Simon, with a beaming face, leaned down and kissed me. "You know I love you. And if you want, I will tell you a thousand times a day."

As Simon straightened, Gene took his place and kissed me as well on the mouth with a murmured, "Precious one, you are my one and only wish."

Oh, that was pretty, and tears pricked my eyes. But still they continued to dress. Not exactly the reaction I'd pictured. What happened to showering me with some loving? "May I ask where you're going in such a hurry?" I said, miffed.

"Going to get color swatches," Simon announced.

"Packing up your stuff and moving it," chimed in Gene.

I laughed at them both. "Get back here, both of you. Simon, while I appreciate your willingness to let me put my mark on our home, it doesn't need to be done right this minute. And for what I have planned, Gene, clothes won't be necessary." I crooked my finger, spread my thighs, and smiled.

Then laughed again as, in their eagerness to comply with my wishes, they ruined yet another set of their clothes.

Perhaps I should learn to sew? Nah. Maybe I'd just learn to stay naked.

## EPILOGUE

As it turned out, Simon and Gene ended up not letting me out of bed for a week, although I was allowed to check in with my best friends by phone in between bouts. Did I mention I'd never felt better or smiled more?

Reality eventually intruded in the form of my promise to Limbo tugging at me. I'd told the boys about my deal with the entity that wasn't exactly alive—and who boggled the mind—and how I'd promised I'd kind of rule over it.

My task? To ensure that the balance was kept between good and evil. My lovers didn't look surprised and declared they knew that, as the first hybrid misfit, I was destined for great things. My reply was a large snort.

They didn't require any coaxing to move, much to my surprise, and they immediately called up some dwarven architects to start designing plans for the grandest palace ever. I would have argued that a hut would do so long as I had them, but seriously, a palace, how cool was that?

The moment I returned to Limbo, clasped in Simon's

arms—I didn't want to disappoint him by telling him my bond with the place allowed me to move to and fro with ease—I looked upon the changed landscape, my soon-to-be-home, and smiled.

For so long I'd fought and wandered, trying to find my place in the world, and as it turned out, I'd needed to create it. *And it's beautiful, if I do say so myself,* I thought, looking around with pride at the lush landscape forged from my blood and promise.

"So what are you going to call it?" Gene asked, hugging me from behind. "Limbo seems kind of outdated now."

Funny he should mention it, for I'd already given the subject some thought. "Well, as the first hybrid misfit and queen or empress or whatever you want to call me of this land, how's Misfitia, a place where anyone is welcome, no matter how different they may be."

Simon rumbled, "I like it," and Gene, with a flourish of his hands and an impressive smoke display that made me cough, gave me a present.

When the fumes cleared, I laughed as I saw what he'd done for me. He'd created my very own Stonehenge and etched in a massive rock for all to see:

*Welcome to Misfitia, ruled by Beth, High Queen of all the Misfits.*

"You forgot one thing," I said, linking my arm through both of theirs. "Where's 'along with her beloved consorts, Simon and Gene, for all of eternity'?"

Apparently, adjustments to my sign would wait, for with expressions that bespoke of their love for me, my dragon and genie proved to me in the soft grass of my new land just how much they liked the idea—and then proved it again.

### THE END
### STAY TUNED FOR LANA'S STORY NEXT.

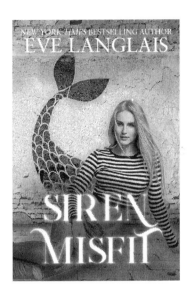

### MORE BOOKS AT EVELANGLAIS.COM

Printed in Poland
by Amazon Fulfillment
Poland Sp. z o.o., Wrocław

53546225R00096